# Millie's Grand Adventure

## BOOK SIX

of the
*A Life of Faith:
Millie Keith*
Series

Based on the beloved books by
Martha Finley

MCP
**Mission City Press**

Franklin, Tennessee

Book Six of the *A Life of Faith: Millie Keith* Series

Millie's Grand Adventure
Copyright © 2002, Mission City Press, Inc. All Rights Reserved.

Published by Mission City Press, Inc.

This book is based on the *Mildred Keith* novels written by Martha Finley and first published in 1876 by Dodd, Mead & Company.

Adaptation Written by:      Kersten Hamilton
Cover & Interior Design:    Richmond & Williams
Cover Photography:          Michelle Grisco Photography
Typesetting:                BookSetters

Unless otherwise indicated, all Scripture references are from the Holy Bible, New International Version (NIV). Copyright © 1973, 1978, 1984 by International Bible Society. Used by permission of Zondervan Publishing House, Grand Rapids, MI. All rights reserved.

*Millie Keith* and *A Life of Faith* are trademarks of Mission City Press, Inc.

For more information, write to Mission City Press at 202 Second Avenue South, Franklin, Tennessee 37064, or visit our Web Site at: **www.alifeoffaith.com.**

**For a FREE catalog call 1-800-840-2641.**

Library of Congress Catalog Card Number: 2002103830
Finley, Martha
        Millie's Grand Adventure
        Book Six of the *A Life of Faith: Millie Keith* Series
        Hardcover:      ISBN-10: 1-928749-14-3
                        ISBN-13: 978-1-928749-14-1
        Softcover:      ISBN-10: 1-928749-46-1
                        ISBN-13: 978-1-928749-46-2

Printed in the United States of America
6 7 8 9 10 11 — 12 11 10 09 08

# DEDICATION

This book is
dedicated to
the memory of
## MARTHA FINLEY
## 1828—1909

*Martha Finley was a woman of God
clearly committed to advancing the cause of Christ
through stories of people who sought
to reflect Christian character in everyday life.
Although written in an era very different from ours,
her works still inspire both young and old
to seek to know and follow the living God.*

# — FOREWORD —

*W*elcome to *Millie's Grand Adventure*, the sixth book in *A Life of Faith: Millie Keith* Series. Millie Keith, our charming heroine, has come a long way in her adventure with God that began four years earlier when she found out that she would be moving to the frontier. She has blossomed physically and emotionally, and so has her life of faith.

Our story resumes in the summer of 1837, as the Keith family prepares for a lean winter in Pleasant Plains. Millie Keith is seeking God's will for her future and His plan for her life. Through heartaches and miracles, Millie will learn to lay her own will down and follow Jesus, no matter where He leads.

The stories of Millie Keith, known formerly as the *Mildred Keith* novels, were written by Martha Finley and released in 1876, eight years after Miss Finley's well-known Elsie Dinsmore books were introduced. This book is an adaptation of the original story. The plot has been significantly expanded, and new characters have been added and existing ones have been more fully developed. The goal was to help readers get a deeper look into the life and heart of Millie.

## ∾ THE CHRISTIAN CALL ∾

It sometimes seems that Christians of the past had an easier time living for Jesus, but in Millie Keith's days it was very difficult indeed. Just one generation after the Second Great Awakening, the spiritual state of America was appalling. In 1835 only one of every eight Americans attended church, and society reflected this. The nation was

iv

# *Foreword*

on the brink of the great westward movement to the final frontier, and the Holy Spirit was working on the hearts of men and women to make a choice about their own lives as well as the direction their nation was to take.

Charles Finney, a firebrand preacher credited with being instrumental in the salvation of 500,000 people, was preaching a radical turn to God, both for the individual and for the nation. Christianity had to embrace both the Great Commandment and the Great Commission. Christians must not only love God with all their heart, mind, soul, and strength; they must also love their neighbor as themselves by telling them of Jesus and teaching them His ways.

*The Christian Spectator* summed it up this way: "The grand result to which revivals are here tending, is the complete moral innovation of the world." Christians were called to improve the intellectual, spiritual, and social condition of mankind.

Finney urged new converts to become involved in "abolition of slavery, temperance, moral reform, politics, business principles, physiological and dietetic reform."

## ∾ SOCIAL REFORM ∾

Temperance was a grave issue for Christians. Alcohol played an important role in politics, religion, and medicine, as well as in social functions. Many people believed that alcohol was necessary for maintaining strength for heavy labor. During the 1830s Americans fifteen years old and older consumed on average between 6.6 and 7.1 gallons of alcohol per year. As a result of the temperance movements, however, by 1845 they consumed just 1.8 gallons per year.

v

# Millie's Great Adventure

Although there were great successes, there were failures as well. Many Christians rallied to the call for abolition, or the complete abolishment of slavery, but the church did not do so well in standing up for another persecuted people: the Native Americans. During the 1830s they were moved out of their homelands and pushed west into barren, desolate lands so that white men could take over the lands they were leaving. By 1837 the last of the Indians were gone from Indiana, and other states were sending the tribes west as well.

In 1831, the Creek Indians of Alabama sent two chiefs to Washington to ask for protection for their people from the invading white settlers. "They bring spirits among us for the purpose of practicing fraud," the chiefs said. "They daily rob us of our property; they bring white officers among us, and take our property from us for debts we never contracted. . . . We have made many treaties with the United States, at all times with the belief that the making was to be the last."

Sadly, it was never the last. As white settlers needed land, the Indians were abused, then pushed off their land once again. In 1838, the state of Georgia declared that Cherokee Indians must be out of the state by May. Soldiers with bayonets searched out every man, woman, and child. The Cherokee had adopted many of the white man's ways—they lived in comfortable homes and farmed just as their neighbors did. Now their houses were confiscated, and they were left with nothing but the clothes on their backs. Fifteen thousand Cherokee people began to move west on foot, by horse, or by wagon, escorted by federal troops. Cherokee ministers asked that the march be halted each Sabbath. They erected pulpits and preached the Word of God just as they would have in their home churches. When they camped by rivers, they would have baptisms.

Having left their homes with nothing, they were forced to beg from churches they passed. To reach the land they had been given by the government required two months of travel by foot. Four thousand Cherokee, many of them small children and the elderly, died along the way. The march came to be known as the Trail of Tears. Many years later a soldier from Georgia wrote: "I fought through the Civil War and have seen men shot to pieces and slaughtered by the thousands, but the Cherokee removal was the cruelest work I ever knew."

Of all the Indian Nations, the only people to fight the forced exodus were the Seminoles, who fought for their land in the swamps of the Florida Everglades. They were finally allowed to keep the land since the white settlers could not farm it.

## ✎ THE MISSIONS MOVEMENT ✎

Churches and missions societies sent workers to the poor in the cities, to the new immigrants arriving from Europe, and even to the slaves on plantations in the South. In the 1830s a new missions field opened: the West.

Mountain men had been trapping beaver in the Rocky Mountains for years, selling the pelts at a yearly rendezvous. They told stories of fertile lands and open meadows, lands so rich a farmer could grow two crops in a year . . . but they were known for weaving tall tales. The beaver pelts were used to make beaver hats, a high-fashion item. But fashions change, and by the mid-1830s the fur trade was dying.

In 1835, the Methodist Church sent Jason Lee and three other Christian men to the Indian tribes to "live with them, learn their language, preach Christ to them, and as the way opens, to introduce schools, agriculture, and the arts of civilized life." The Catholic Church had sent missionaries and priests as far west as California for centuries, but Jason Lee preached the first Protestant sermon west of the Rockies. Lee and the others traveled with fur traders.

## ∾ WESTWARD HO! ∾

Another young missionary, Dr. Marcus Whitman, traveled west with Jim Bridger, the famous explorer and mountain man. Whitman later returned to the west, determined to bring settlers over the mountains to the Oregon Territory. People believed the young missionary when he spoke of the richness of the land and the need of the Indians to hear the Gospel, but he could convince very few to go with him.

Life on the frontier was hard—the struggle to survive left little time for "book learning" and socializing. Men and women plowed the fields and hunted for food. Fish was a staple of many diets. In Indiana, settlers gathered walnuts and hickory nuts, grapes, and many kinds of wild berries. They hunted and fished.

One family alone in the woods of Indiana would have to live off the food they could grow, the berries and nuts they could gather, and the meat they could hunt. In a small community they could barter: if one farmer raised pigs, he could trade pork to another for wheat or apples. The standard of living was raised as each family contributed. As towns grew, life became easier. Money could be made by logging and farming. A dry goods store would carry sugar, molasses, raisins, cheese, salted meats, tea, coffee, and dried beans, as well as tools, nails, shoes, clothing, and

fabric — all the supplies needed to build a life. People who had founded towns and worked to make them grow were not likely to relocate to an even wilder frontier. But something happened that opened the gates of the westward tide. It came in 1837, in the form of an economic crash.

## ∾ THE CRASH OF 1837 ∾

After the second war with England (1812–1814), government land had been sold for paper money. Millions of acres were bought on credit by private individuals and land speculators. In 1836, the "Specie Circular" issued by President Andrew Jackson and the Secretary of the Treasury required payment for government lands to be made in gold and silver. Property everywhere was sacrificed, and prices declined. Then, like an avalanche, came a business crash. Thousands of people faced financial ruin in 1837. During the first three weeks of April, 250 business houses failed in New York alone. Every sector of the economy was involved: the mechanic, the farmer, the laborer, the lawyer. Bankruptcy was commonplace, and even the federal government could not pay its debts. Out of 850 banks in the nation, 343 closed and 62 failed partially. People lost their businesses and their homes. They began to look to the western lands for new hope and a new beginning. With the crash, the bottom finally fell out of the pelt market, and the mountain men found new work leading a growing stream of settlers over the mountains they knew so well. This stream eventually became a flood, with more than 350,000 people migrating to Oregon or California between 1840 and 1870. By 1890 the American frontier was gone.

# Millie's Great Adventure

America has no frontier to pursue and develop anymore, but men and women are still faced with the choice of how they will live their lives. Every Christian is called to obey the Great Commandment and the Great Commission. Will you live for Jesus or for yourself? Will you have the courage to stand up for what is right before God, as Millie did when she helped Luke and Laylie escape and when she turned down Charles's marriage proposal because he was not a believer in the Lord?

One day the history books will record how well our generation carried out the commands of Jesus. What do you think they will say? How can you live the Great Commandment and the Great Commission in your life? That is today's frontier for each one of us. Through Jesus we can advance God's Kingdom, just as Millie did.

# KEITH FAMILY TREE

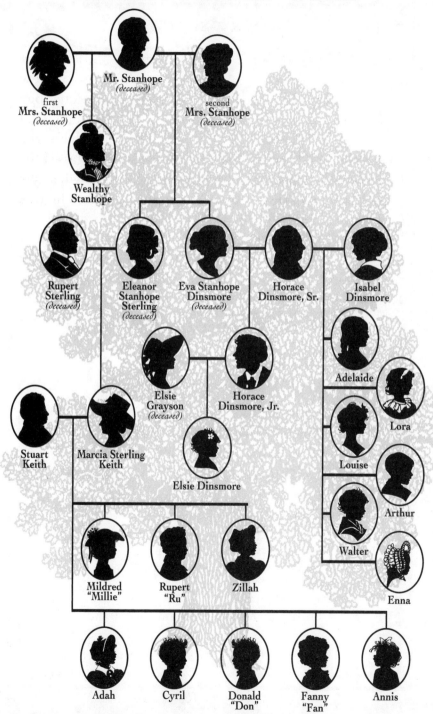

# SETTING

*O*ur story begins in the summer of 1837 in Pleasant Plains, Indiana, the hometown of Millie Keith and her family.

# CHARACTERS

## ∞ THE KEITH FAMILY ∞

**Stuart Keith**—the father of the Keith family and a respected attorney-at-law.

**Marcia Keith**—the mother of the Keith family and the step-niece of Aunt Wealthy Stanhope.

**The Keith children:**

> **Mildred Eleanor ("Millie")**—age 16
>
> **Rupert ("Ru")**—age 15
>
> **Zillah**—age 13
>
> **Adah**—age 12
>
> **Cyril** and **Donald ("Don")**—age 11, twin boys
>
> **Fanny ("Fan")**—age 9
>
> **Annis**—age 5

## ∞ PLEASANT PLAINS, INDIANA ∞

**Mrs. Lightcap and her children:**

> **Gordon**—age 20; he is the hostler and blacksmith at the local stagecoach station and a close friend of the Keiths.

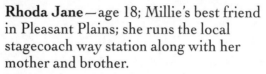

**Rhoda Jane**—age 18; Millie's best friend in Pleasant Plains; she runs the local stagecoach way station along with her mother and brother.

**Emmaretta**—age 12

**Minerva ("Min")**—age 10

**Reverend Matthew and Celestia Ann Lord**— a local minister and his wife.

**Dr. and Mrs. Chetwood**—the town physician and his wife.

**William ("Bill")**—age 18

**Claudina**—age 17

**Mr. and Mrs. Grange**—the bank president and his wife.

**Lucilla ("Lu")**—age 18

**Teddy**—age 12

**Mr. and Mrs. Monocker**—the owner of the local mercantile store and his wife.

**York**—age 20

**Helen**—age 19

**Mr. and Mrs. Ormsby**—a local businessman and his wife.

**Wallace**—age 20

**Sally**—age 9

**Mr. and Mrs. Roe**—local farmers.

**Beth**—age 18

**Nicholas Ransquate** and his wife **Damaris Drybread Ransquate**—friends of the Keiths.

**Mrs. Prescott**—a widowed neighbor.

**Mrs. Prior**—the landlady of the Union Hotel.

**Mrs. Simon**—an elderly widow.

**Toby**—a neighborhood boy.

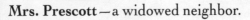

### ∞ Others ∞

**Gavriel Mikolaus ("Gavi")**—a gypsy, age 20, with two younger siblings:

> **Jedidiah ("Jed")**—age 9
>
> **Jasmine ("Jaz")**—age 5

**Charles Landreth**—age 21; a friend of the Dinsmore family and nephew to the Landreths; he met Millie on her trip to Roselands and asked her to marry him.

**Rayme Romanik**—a young Romani man.

**Augustus Romanik**—Rayme's grandfather.

# PROLOGUE

# Prologue

*illie Keith is home at last, after spending nearly a year at Roselands. The trip to the South was trying to her faith and to her soul. Her courage had been tested by the cruelties of slavery, and her relationship with her uncle Horace Dinsmore was broken when she helped two slave children belonging to his wife's family escape. Millie had left the South disgraced in the eyes of her relations, but stronger than ever in her faith. And she had left very much in love with Charles Landreth.*

*God seemed to take a hand in her affairs once again when Millie met an older girl named Gavriel—a girl with the courage to stop a runaway stage, a haunting secret in her past, and a younger brother and sister to care for. Gavi was traveling to Lansdale to live with Millie's own Aunt Wealthy Stanhope! When they found Aunt Wealthy's house quarantined, Stuart and Marcia Keith stayed to help fight the sickness, and Gavi traveled on with Millie to help her care for the big house at Keith Hill until Millie's parents could return. Now the Keiths are together once more, cleaning up from a terrible storm and preparing for the lean winter ahead.*

*tuart had winked at his wife when he offered to read to the children, and Marcia had taken Millie's hand and they slipped out the door.

"You did a good job, Millie," Marcia said when Millie stopped at last. "I'm very proud of you."

"I didn't, Mamma. I know I couldn't keep the house from almost blowing down, but Cyril smoked cigars, Fan thought she was turning into a cow, Don and Cyril had a fistfight, and Zillah has fallen in love with the sheriff. All of it springs from their hearts — the very part that I was not caring for! I'm sure I'm never going to have children of my own. I'm not wise enough, and I'm afraid I never will be."

Mamma laughed. "Nonsense. The Lord in His wisdom first sends us babies — not twelve year olds. By the time you have a son who smokes cigars or a daughter in love with the sheriff, you will have had years and years of practice in training them up in the Lord, and you will be much more mature in the Lord, too."

"The worst part was questions I couldn't answer," Millie said. "Gavriel asked if the promises of the Bible are for all of us, and I didn't know how to answer her. She has had such a hard life. And Cyril — he asked me to prove that God was real. I knew the Scriptures, but . . . " She shook her head and sighed heavily.

"We can tell people about our dear Lord," Marcia said. "We can tell them what He has done, and we can show them His love. But in the end, God Himself comes to meet each of His children. He is the only one who can prove Himself, Millie."

"Like He did to Cyril," responded Millie.

"Like He did to Cyril," Marcia said with conviction. "Each of us has our own special love story with God — the story of how He proved Himself to us, how He came into our lives. I do know part of the answer for Gavriel — God's promises *are* for each and every one of His children. But I don't know the adventure He has planned for her. I only know that it will be good, because He is good."

"I think I may know part of His good plan for her," Millie said with a smile. She looked up to see Gordon Lightcap coming up the road, a bouquet in his hands.

# Prologue

"Good evening, ladies," he said. "May I escort you home?"

"Are those flowers for me?" Marcia teased.

"No, ma'am," Gordon said, "though I'll bring you some tomorrow, if you like. I've had a certain young lady on my mind for a while, and I'm thinking it's time I say something about it."

"I see!" Marcia smiled. "Then I suggest we go up to the house."

Everyone looked up as they came in. Gordon walked straight up to Gavi and held out the flowers. "Miss Mikolaus," he began, but he never finished the sentence. Gavi put her hands over her face and ran from the room.

~

"Gavi?" Millie knocked on the bedroom door Gavi had shut behind her. "May I come in? If you want to talk . . . "

"Come in," called a faint voice. Millie pushed the door open, peering cautiously around until she could see into the room. Gavi was busy throwing things into her trunk.

"Surely you're not leaving?" Millie asked, puzzled. "Gavi . . . whatever it is, we can talk about it. I . . . I truly want to be your friend. And Mamma and Pappa are eager for you to stay on with us. This is a good place for Jedidiah and Jaz; you've said so yourself. And Gordon—"

"Gordon is the reason I have to leave," Gavi said, looking up for the first time since Millie had entered the room. The haunted look had returned to her beautiful, dark eyes, and tears had gathered in them. "I could fall in love with him so easily . . . " she started, her voice catching in a sob.

# Millie's Great Adventure

"I'm sure that Gordon would love you too," Millie said, taking a step toward her friend. "You would make him so happy."

"Oh, *please* don't say that," Gavi sobbed. "Gordon Lightcap is the most wonderful man I have ever met. But I can't love him, Millie. I can't. I'm a married woman!"

# Hopes Dashed

*For the grace of God.... teaches us to say "No" to ungodliness and worldly passions, and to live self-controlled, upright and godly lives in this present age, while we wait for the blessed hope....*

TITUS 2:11–13

*M*arried!" Millie Keith sank slowly onto the guest room chair, watching in disbelief as her friend threw blouses, petticoats, and pantalets into her trunk without bothering to fold them. "Gavi, slow down! Tell me what this is about!"

"Oh, Millie." Gavi's dark eyes were huge. "I never meant to lead Gordon on. You know I didn't!"

*She's right.* Millie thought back over the past weeks, the moonlight dance when Gavi would not step onto the floor with Gordon, the times when she had turned away from him. She had not led him on. But what could poor Gordon be thinking? He'd given his heart away once before, to Claudina Chetwood. She had vowed that she loved him in return—until an accident had left him with a crippled hand. *Lord*—Millie threw a quick prayer heavenward—*help Gordon. Hold his heart in Your hands. Don't let him be hurt again.*

"I should never have come here," Gavi said, seeing the look on Millie's face.

"Yes, you should," Millie said, trying to sound firm. "My Aunt Wealthy would call our meeting a divine appointment. I couldn't have managed these last weeks without you." It was true. Keeping the big house on Keith Hill running smoothly was more than Millie could have done alone.

"How could it be a divine appointment?" Gavi shut the lid of her trunk. "I have deceived you, Millie, and your parents as well. I told you that I had no one to turn to, but that is not the truth. I led you to believe that I could not pay for a stage ticket. That was not exactly true, either, although . . ." She put her hand to her head. "It's all so complica—*hic*. Oh, no! I will not hiccup, and I will not cry!" Gavi attempted to swallow a sob and hiccup at the same time. Millie moved quickly to her side and put an arm around her. "I *hic* have to be strong. Jedidiah and Jasmine are depending on *hic* me!"

"You are the strongest girl I have ever met," Millie said. "But surely God did not make us to stand alone. Even Jesus asked His friends to pray for Him!"

Gavi shivered. "I wish I were as strong as you seem to think I am," she said. "I do owe your parents an apology, and Gordon as well. Oh, Millie, is he still here? I don't think I can do this more than once. Promise you will stay with me every minute or my courage will fail. *Hic.*"

"I promise," Millie said, taking Gavi's hand. Gavi hesitated at the head of the stairs.

"Go down quietly," she pleaded, "and peek in. Tell me if Gordon is still here." They came down the stairs on tiptoes, and Millie peeked through the parlor door.

All seven of Millie's brothers and sisters were still gathered in the parlor, although Stuart was no longer reading. A lesser room would have been bursting at the seams, but Stuart and Marcia Keith enjoyed their large family, and had planned their home accordingly.

Gavi's brother, Jedidiah, was on the floor with Cyril and Don, the Keith twins, concentrating on the marbles in a ring drawn with chalk on the wooden floor. Fan watched them intently, her arms around the neck of Bobforshort, the short-tailed hound dog. Bob had been given to the twins, and to Don's complete disgust, the dog's heart had settled on Fan and Cyril, not on him. Zillah and Adah were talking quietly as they brushed the little girls' hair and twisted it into braids, gold ones for Annis, jet black for Jaz, Gavi's little sister.

4

Rupert, the most studious of the Keith children, sat quietly in a chair, studying a medical text he had borrowed from Doc Chetwood. *Where are Mamma and Pappa?* Millie leaned a little farther so that she could see the far end of the room. Her parents were talking earnestly with Gordon Lightcap by the fireplace.

"*Hic!*" Gavi clapped her hand over her mouth an instant too late. Everyone looked up. Millie gave her friend's hand a squeeze and pulled her through the door.

"I . . ." Gordon said, paling at the sight of Gavi's tear-stained face. "I'd best be going."

"Please, *hic!*" The hiccup bounced back from the ceiling corners. Gavi looked at Millie in panic. "What I mean to say is, please stay a moment," Gavi said. "I have some *hic*-splaining to do."

Ru looked from Gordon to Gavi and set his book aside. "Come on, Cyril, Don. It's time for bed. I'll say prayers with you tonight."

"It is not time yet." Cyril's wild red hair bounced like springs as he shook his head.

"Yeah," Fan agreed. "What I want to know is—"

Marcia laid her hand on her daughter's head. "All you need to know right now, dear, is that my children are going to bed."

"But what I want to know is, why does Gavi have the hiccups?"

"What *I* want to know," Stuart said in his deep Pappa voice, "is if you can remember a Bible verse about obeying your Mamma?"

Fan's brow puckered.

"Commandment five," Cyril coached her in a loud whisper. "Honor your father and mother."

# Millie's Great Adventure

"Is honor the same as obey?" Fan asked.

"Obeying your parents is one way to honor them," Stuart said, looking stern. "I think your memory verse for this evening should be Ephesians 6:1. 'Children, obey your parents in the Lord, for this is right.' And you will recite it also, Cyril. Put Bob out before you go upstairs."

"Yes, Pappa."

Zillah stood with Annis in her arms. "I'll help you put the children to bed, Mamma."

Jedidiah looked hopefully at his older sister, but she nodded. "You two go to bed as well."

The children trooped out of the room, Cyril dragging Bob by his rope collar. The back door opened and shut, and Millie put her hands over her ears. During her parents' absence Fan had sneaked the hound upstairs to sleep under her bed; now every evening when he was banished to the porch, he gave out one long, brokenhearted howl before curling up on his own bed by the door.

When Bob had finished his lament, Gavi settled into a straight-backed chair. She folded her hands in her lap and fixed her eyes on them, occasionally lifting her eyes to the face of the grandfather clock. Millie pulled a chair close enough to sit by her friend and patted her hands now and then.

Stuart kept Gordon occupied with questions about the stage station stables and the horses he cared for there, but the young man's eyes kept drifting to Gavi. The tick-tock-*hic* of passing time was just becoming unbearable when Marcia came back into the sitting room carrying a tea tray.

"There," she said, pouring Gavi a cup of steaming golden liquid. "Chamomile tea always helps me when I have the hiccups."

Gavi took the cup gratefully. "Mr. and Mrs. Keith," she began, after taking a sip of tea, "everyone has been so busy working to put things back in order after the storm that I haven't had a chance to properly *hic* thank you for taking us in. I have some explaining to do, and an apology to make to you, Mr. Lightcap."

"I'm sure you haven't done anything wrong," Gordon said.

"I in no way intended to lead you on," Gavi said with a blush. "You offered honest affections, but I have been dishonest. I cannot accept them because I am a married woman."

Gordon looked as if he had been slapped. Stuart's eyebrows went up, and Marcia said, "Oh, dear!" as she set her teacup down with a distinct clink.

"You know that I am a Romani," Gavi went on. "Our customs are different from yours. When I was nine years old, I was married to a young man of my clan."

"Nine! But that's no older than Fan!" Millie said. "How could you possibly marry?" She was sorry at once for the outburst, as Gavi looked down at her clenched hands once more.

"How can you understand? You know nothing of our ways."

"Allow us the privilege of learning," Stuart said, settling beside his wife on the couch. "We may not be Romani, but we are in Christ, and so are you. Surely that is stronger than any earthly tie?"

Gavi nodded, eyes still downcast.

"I want you to know that you had our forgiveness as soon as you asked," Marcia said. "And you are welcome in our home, even if you choose to tell us no more."

# Millie's Great Adventure

Millie was amazed at the calming effect of her mother's words. Gavi's face softened and relaxed, and she dared to look up again.

"I do want to tell you," she said at last. "I haven't had anyone to talk to in so long. There are not so many of us in the Americas, you know." She took a sip of tea. Her hiccups seemed to have vanished as Marcia had promised. "Rom marry Rom. A Romani man who marries a *gadji*, a woman who is not Rom, may be forgiven, but a Romani woman may never marry a *gadjo*. A woman would never be forgiven for such a thing.

"My father had an acquaintance, Augustus Romanik, just over from the old country. He had a grandson of fifteen—Rayme." Gavriel's voice softened as she spoke the name, and Millie could not help but think of Charles Landreth and the way her own heart skipped at the sound of his name. "There was no horse Rayme couldn't ride, no contest he couldn't win. He could sing, and play the violin, banjo, or guitar." Gavi smiled at the memory. "He made cards disappear and eggs appear in their place. I asked him how he did it, and he said there was magic in his hands."

"Might I ask which old country your family came from?" Stuart asked. Millie was sure he had changed the subject for Gordon's sake. The young man was massaging his twisted hand, his eyes fixed on the far wall.

*Magic in his hands. Gordon might have said that about his own hands, once. Before his right hand was shattered and twisted.*

"I should have said 'countries.'" Gavi hadn't noticed Gordon's discomfort. "We claim them all, but no country wants to claim us. My family, as well as Rayme's, came most recently from the Basque Mountains in Spain." She took

another sip of tea. "Our marriage was arranged in the tra-
ditional way, with days of arguing over my bride price. 'She
is no cook,' Mr. Romanik would say. 'Ah, but she can train
horses almost as well as her mother, and her mother is making me a rich man.' Father showed a pocket full of coins to
prove it. Finally they drank the wine of agreement, and Mr.
Romanik fastened a heavy necklace around my neck." She
set down her teacup, as if this were the end of the story.

"A necklace?" Millie prompted.

"It meant that an agreement had been made. I belonged
to Rayme, and no one else could marry me. Rom aren't
married by preachers or judges. It's the agreement that
matters. A simple ceremony of exchanging bread was all
that was left. It was set for a week later, so the families
could attend. It stormed that day. The last relative to arrive
was my mother's mother, Granmarie, and it seemed that
thunder and lightning came through the door with her, and
right into the room. Mr. Romanik spat when he saw her.

" 'Manners as lovely as ever, I see,' Granmarie said. 'Let's
take a little walk, shall we, Augustus?'

"He followed her outside, into the storm. We all crowded
around the windows to watch. Mr. Romanik swung his
arms, and blustered until I thought that Granmarie would
be blown away, but she pointed one finger at him, jabbing
it like a pin into a bladder balloon as she spoke. The puff
and rumble seemed to leak out of him."

"What did she say?" Millie asked, fascinated in spite of
herself.

Gavi spread her hands. "I don't know. Romani women
do not have much power, but Granmarie was different. She
had met a woman named Wealthy Stanhope in
Philadelphia." Stuart and Marcia glanced at each other.

"And it had changed her life. Granmarie was fearless when she believed in her cause. 'Pack a bag,' she told me. 'You are going with me to Philly.'

" 'What about my grandson?' Mr. Romanik asked.

" 'Don't be ridiculous, Augustus,' Granmarie said. 'You have to keep him yourself.'

" 'I mean'—and he was bellowing again—'when can he come to Philadelphia?'

" 'He can come to Philly when Gavi is sixteen.'

" 'And retrieve his wife?'

" 'And we will *talk*,' Granmarie said. Even my mother gasped at her boldness, but no one stopped us.

"Granmarie and I moved to Philadelphia. She taught me to read the Bible and many other books. I learned more of music and art and grew to love my life with her. On my sixteenth birthday . . . Rayme . . . didn't come." Her voice was quiet. "He never came. We heard that he had left his grandfather and was making his own way in the world. My parents left the road and moved in with us for a time; Jedidiah attended school. My father was killed in a shipyard accident just before Jaz was born. And then the typhoid came. It took them both, Granmarie and Mother, in one terrible week. Only one Romani came to the funeral—Grandfather Romanik. He walked to the front of the church and slapped her coffin.

" 'Who's laughing now, Marie?' he said. 'It is I, Augustus Romanik. I am alive, and I am laughing. I win, Marie.' "

Millie shuddered at the thought. *No wonder Gavi's eyes are haunted!*

Gavi shrugged. "But he didn't win. I took Jed and Jaz, and we slipped out the back of the church. Our bags were already packed, so we went straight to the stage station. I

# Hopes Dashed

used Granmarie's money to buy tickets. We have looked for Rayme ever since, and Augustus looks for us."

"Why would Augustus follow you?" Marcia asked. "Surely he knows you would just leave again."

"He doesn't want us," Gavi said simply. "He wants this." She pulled something from her pocket, and Millie gasped. Burnished gold glinted in the firelight. "My betrothal necklace," Gavi said, jingling the coins on their thick golden links.

"May I?" Millie took the necklace, and turned a coin to the fire to see the head better. "Gavi, this is Julius Caesar!"

"And a few of his brothers, cousins, and nephews, I presume," Gavi said, as Millie handed the treasure back. "The Rom are an old people, and this has been in the Romanik family for a very long time. Now it's mine—mine and Rayme's. It's our future. Or it will be, when I find him."

Marcia opened her mouth to say something, then closed it again. Stuart was rubbing his temples, as he did when deep in thought.

"Miss . . . Mrs. Romanik." The sound of Gordon's voice made Millie jump. He had been sitting so quietly she had forgotten him entirely. "I'll find him. I'll find Rayme Romanik for you."

"I couldn't ask—"

"You don't have to," Gordon said. "The Bible tells us to treat young ladies as our sisters. If Rhoda Jane's husband was missing, I'd go and find him."

"It's . . . it's a very kind offer, but I . . . I need time to think and to pray," Gavi said. Marcia gave the girl a pleased look.

"An excellent suggestion," Stuart said.

For the next hour, the Keiths' parlor resembled the heavenly throne room more than a frontier home, as prayers and petitions were laid at the feet of the King of Kings. Finally Gavi went to her room, pleading exhaustion. Gordon said his good-byes, and Stuart and Marcia stood with their arms around each other.

"What do you think?" Stuart asked.

"I think Gordon's in love with that young lady."

"And she's in love with another," Stuart sighed. "Poor Gordon."

"I wonder," Marcia said, then shook her head. "Are you ready for bed, Millie?"

"I believe I'll sit here for a few more moments," Millie said, kissing her parents good night.

Gordon's wilted flowers lay forgotten in the chimney corner. Millie picked them up. She couldn't save the delicate blooms from drying and turning to dust, any more than she could pull Gordon's heart from the fire of love. There was something fine in Gordon Lightcap—a faith that time could not burn up, a hope in something beyond what he could taste and hear and feel. Gordon would do what was right simply because it was right, and never count the cost to himself.

*Why didn't Rayme come to the funeral? Why didn't he come for Gavi? Nothing would have stopped Gordon Lightcap from coming to her,* Millie was sure. *Let Gavi's husband be a worthy man,* she prayed. *Let him be worth the sacrifice my dear friend is willing to make for him. Oh, Lord, how can this turn out right?*

Millie lifted her head and sat in the still calm for a few minutes, her eyes going from one end of the room to the other. Then she picked up a coal-oil lamp to light the way to her room. Once there, she set the lamp on her dressing table, lifted the lid of the pretty tin box, and took out a dried red rose. *Charles Landreth.* She couldn't touch the long-dry flower without an ache in her heart. Charles had given it to

12

her just before his final proposal. Just before she'd turned him down. She set it carefully on the tabletop, then unfolded the letter she kept in the box beneath it.

*Dearest, Dearest Millie,*

*Ha! I can just imagine your face as you read that greeting. There's nothing you can do about my calling you that, after all. You are a thousand miles away . . . You should know that you are no less troublesome at a distance of a thousand miles. I would much rather that you were here so that I could look into those big blue eyes and say, "Millie, you have mud behind your ears," or perhaps "there is spinach stuck in your teeth."*

Millie smiled. She had felt like—no, she had been—a walking disaster around Charles Landreth. Things just seemed to *happen* when he was about, no matter how hard she tried to be proper, prim, and above scandal or reproach.

*I'm reading your book.*

The Bible she had left with him was tattered and worn, but it was God's Word. *It's not my book at all, Lord,* she prayed, *it's Yours. You have promised that faith comes by hearing, and hearing by the Word of God. I have done my best to tell Charles about You. I've done my best to show him who You are. Now it's up to You. Please, Lord! Reveal Yourself to Charles as he reads. And send someone to speak to Rayme, as well. Reveal Yourself to them, Lord.*

She put the letter and the rose away carefully and opened her prayer journal.

*August*—she wrote the date neatly at the top of the page, then held the nib over the paper so long she had to dip it again before she could write.

13

# Millie's Great Adventure

*Dear Father,* she wrote. *I hope You won't consider this impertinent, but perhaps You should reconsider one aspect of Your creation. I'm not sure romance is necessary at all. In fact, it causes no end of trouble.*

The rest of the page was a terrible blank whiteness, made foglike by the tears in her eyes. Millie blinked them away. *Just like my future, and Gavi's and Gordon's. A blank page and a blank book. Can't You tell me how this will end, Lord?*

She put her head down on her arms so the tears wouldn't run off her nose.

# CHAPTER

**2**

# Wise Counsel

*Choose my instruction instead of silver, knowledge rather than choice gold, for wisdom is more precious than rubies, and nothing you desire can compare with her.*

PROVERBS 8:10–11

illie awoke and pulled her clothes on before the sun was up, hoping to catch her mother before anyone else was awake. She was still trying to yawn the cobwebs from her mind as she crept down the stairs. Crying oneself to sleep was not a prescription for sweet dreams and restful slumber.

Millie could hear low laughter before she entered the kitchen. Someone was already up with Marcia.

"Good morning, dear," Marcia said, glancing up from the fire she was lighting in the stove. Stuart filled the teakettle from the bucket of fresh water by the back door.

"I believe you are married to a Proverbs 31 woman, Pappa," Millie said, stifling another yawn. "Up before dawn to care for her family."

"Every palace needs one," Stuart said with a smile.

"What this palace needs is a few logs from the woodpile," Marcia said, checking the woodbox. "Don seems to have neglected his chores."

"And a wife who can make pancakes — she is worth far more than rubies! And her pancakes are worth a trip to the woodpile." Stuart gave a little bow before he went out.

Marcia brought the flour tin from the pantry and dipped four eggs from the soda water in the crockery pot. Millie started measuring the dry ingredients while Marcia separated the eggs.

"Mamma," she said, "I couldn't sleep well last night. Thoughts just kept tumbling through my brain, no matter how I tried to give them to the Lord."

"Would it help to share those thoughts?"

# Millie's Great Adventure

"Some of them, perhaps," Millie said slowly. She didn't know how much she could say about Charles without starting to cry, and her nose simply could not take one more handkerchief. "Some of them were of Gavi. How could Rayme have abandoned her like that?"

Marcia started whipping the egg whites. "It does seem cruel. But we don't know the whole story yet."

"What if he's a horrid man, like his grandfather?" Millie said.

"The Lord didn't create anyone to be horrid, dear. He has good plans for each of us, if only we will follow Him. If Rayme is a Christian man, I am sure things will work out well."

*If he is a Christian man?* Millie hadn't even thought of that, even though Charles's salvation figured so largely in her own hurting heart.

"And if he's not?"

"Then we will pray for him. And pray for Gavi, as well. She seems to be a very mature young lady."

Millie finished mixing the spoonful of lard, baking soda, and salt into the flour, made a well for the milk and eggs, and set the mixture aside. "When do you start to feel grown-up, Mamma? I'm almost seventeen. Old enough to be married, certainly. But I don't feel grown-up. I still have so many questions!"

"I'll tell you a secret," Marcia said, pouring the milk and eggs into the flour and mixing it into a batter. "I still have questions too. I expect I will when I am a gray-haired old lady. You will never have all the answers, Millie. You will always have to seek the Lord and trust Him with things you don't understand. But trusting Him becomes easier the longer you walk with Him, the more you understand how good and faithful He is."

"It's frightening making decisions that will last your whole lifetime," Millie said, sitting on a chair and pulling her knees up to her chin. "It feels as if I'm traveling on an old map with clouds and sea serpents all around the edges, and big letters that read, 'Here there be monsters.' Every decision leads into the blank white mist, and I have no idea what will come next. Do the shivers around the edges go away when you are an adult?"

Marcia looked at her seriously. "No, we do not live in a tame world, and we do not follow a tame Savior. Aunt Wealthy always told me that life was an adventure from the first breath to the last. Being a Christian is trusting that He knows what's in the mists."

"It is so hard to make a decision and then just trust God!"

"Do you mean your decision to turn down Charles's proposal?"

Millie nodded. Marcia put down her wooden spoon and wrapped her arms around her daughter. "You have made very good decisions in the last year, daughter. I am proud of you. You can't imagine what it was like, reading about my daughter's love and not being able to comfort or to hold her. But I knew you would be seeking God. I prayed for you night and day."

"I didn't want to fall in love. If there was any way at all to get him out of my heart, any way at all, I would have done it."

"Love is like that sometimes," Marcia sighed. "As you know, you cannot love someone more than Jesus does. Love is a very special thing, and God does not waste it. If He has allowed you to love this Mr. Landreth, then it is for good, not evil. I have been praying for this young man since the first time you mentioned him in a letter. From everything you have said about him, he seems bright and determined. And I am delighted that he is reading the Bible."

"That's true," Millie said. "But you sound hesitant, Mamma."

"Look." She turned Millie toward the window. Stuart raised the ax and swung. The ax flashed, then sliced into the wood. He picked up the pieces of split log, tossed them to one side, and reached for another log.

"Your father had never lifted an ax until we moved to the frontier, but he came from a hardworking family. Most southern gentlemen could not, or perhaps I should say would not, do that. They have lived with slaves doing the hard work for so many generations that they have come to believe that hard work is beneath them. I remember being told while I was in the South that 'a gentleman must never sweat.' That is simply ridiculous. I'm sure Jesus was the greatest gentleman who ever lived, and I can't imagine that his work as a carpenter never caused him to wipe the sweat from his brow!"

As if hearing their conversation, Stuart pulled his handkerchief from his pocket and mopped his forehead.

Millie laughed. "Pappa is as fine a gentleman as you could ever hope for," she said.

"I agree. And I pray that your young man—whoever he may be—will be like him, willing to work and to serve others."

Millie bit her lip. During her stay at Roselands she had learned how easy it was to let others do the hard work for you. Ladies of good families simply did not do washing or housework of any kind. Her own hands had grown so soft while she was there that sweeping, mopping, and beating rugs had raised blisters when she returned to Pleasant

Plains. Even now they were rough and red from scrubbing laundry on the washboard. Red and rough like Mamma's.

Marcia went back to her pancake batter. Millie watched her hands as she deftly folded in the egg whites. *It wasn't work that made Mamma's hands rough. It was love. Loving her family enough to knead the bread, wash the clothes, make the soap. But what would Charles Landreth think of them if he saw them? He is used to ladies like Isabel Dinsmore, ladies with soft hands that have never done any work at all.* Millie spread her own hands before her. *Charles loved me at Roselands, when I wore silk and dancing slippers. Will he love me still if he sees me in Pleasant Plains?*

"Aunt Wealthy was very wise when your father was courting me," Marcia said gently. "She told me to ask Stuart about his dreams, and if they did not match my own, then let him go. Just being a Christian man was not enough. We not only had to dream well together, we had to work well together. A lifetime is a very long time to spend with someone."

The back door opened and Stuart staggered in under a pile of freshly split wood. It filled the kitchen with a pine forest smell, and in a rush it came over Millie how much she loved the frontier. *If Charles did become a Christian, could she live with him in the South? Would he be able to live with her here?*

Stuart deposited his armload in the woodbox. "Not bad for a lawyer. I believe I have earned those pancakes."

"Stacks of them," Marcia agreed, "dripping with butter and hot maple syrup."

Adah and Zillah came down the stairs with Fan and Annis, and soon the kitchen was full of Keiths and Mikolauses. Ru went out to milk Belle, and Millie took a basket to find any eggs the chickens might have laid. Most of their flock had been killed, the poor little chicks drowned in the downpour and full-grown chickens crushed or simply carried away when a twister had destroyed the henhouse. Millie found two eggs in the hay of the barn, and then spread cracked corn for the three hens. On her way back into the house, she opened the door for Ru, who carried a bucket of milk.

Cyril skidded in the door just as they were sitting down, his damp hair plastered to his head, ears still red from scrubbing.

Stuart bowed his head. "Lord, we thank You for this food, and for this family to share it with. I ask for Your special blessing and direction for Gavi today and for her husband."

"Husband?" Fan's voice was loud in the sudden silence. "Doesn't that mean you are married?"

Suddenly everyone was talking at once.

"How long have you —"

"What's his name?"

"Where's your ring?"

"Forget the ring" — Cyril's voice carried over the rest. "Where's the husband?"

"Children!" Marcia said. "Where are your manners? Gavi is a guest in this house!"

Adah and Zillah clearly wanted to know more, but they dropped their eyes. "Yes, Mamma," Zillah said.

After the meal was finished, Millie said, "I'll clear the table, Mamma. And do the dishes as well."

Marcia smiled at her. "I have a better idea. I think you should take a morning for yourself," she said. "You worked very hard while I was away, and your health is just returned. I don't want to risk a relapse. In fact, if Gavi is willing to let me watch over her brother and sister, I think she should have a day off too."

Gavi hesitated. There were shadows under her eyes, and Millie was sure she had not slept well either. Marcia was right; fresh air and exercise would be good for both of them.

"We could take a walk," Millie suggested.

Gavi glanced at Jed and Jaz, but they didn't seem a bit worried about a day without her. "I'd like that," she said at last.

Stuart put on his coat and kissed his wife and children, stopping to wipe a dab of butter from Annis's chubby face with a napkin before he accepted her kiss.

"Have a good day at the office, Pappa," Millie said.

"Why don't you invite Wallace home for supper tonight?" Marcia suggested. "We haven't seen him for days."

"Yes, Pappa, do," Zillah said; then realizing that everyone was looking at her, she flushed.

"We love Wallace's stories," Millie said, to spare Zillah more embarrassment. "It would be lovely to hear the continuing adventures of our frontier sheriff tonight."

"I'm sure he will be pleased that he is so popular around here." Stuart settled his hat on his head. "As I'm equally sure that your cooking is popular with Wallace, I would suggest you set another plate at the table. If Wallace has the bad fortune to have a previous engagement, I will bring along any poor fellow he has locked up in jail."

"Really, Stuart!" Marcia said. "I hardly think Wallace would allow that."

"He's never had anyone locked up in jail," Don pointed out. "He told me that himself." Jedidiah and Cyril looked disappointed at this news.

"Then I suppose we mustn't get our hopes up," Stuart said. "We will have to settle for the sheriff himself, or no one at all."

As soon as he was out the door, Marcia set about ordering her household for the day. "Adah will care for Annis and Jaz, and Zillah can listen to lessons this morning. I am going to bake some bread for Mrs. Simon. The poor woman is no better now than when I left Pleasant Plains two months ago."

Millie was suddenly twice as thankful that she was going on a walk. God expected charity for all creatures, but surely even He knew Mrs. Simon was not an easy case. If one brought daisies, she developed an allergy on the spot. Fresh bread must not only be delivered, it must be sliced very thin and just brushed with butter. Cow's milk was much too rich for her, although she managed to choke it down. She preferred goat's milk, which someone had assured her was good for what ailed her. Her constant complaining and disagreeable spirit had driven almost every lady of Pleasant Plains away from her door. Only Marcia Keith and the indomitable Mrs. Prior remained.

"Emmett says Mrs. Simon's going to die," Don said, taking the plates from under the cupboard and placing them on the table.

"All the more reason to take good care of her while we have her with us," Marcia said matter-of-factly. "I think we'll make soup as well. Fan, I will need onions and potatoes peeled. You can help with that while the boys work on their mathematics, and they will help when it's your turn."

❦

Millie drew in a delicious breath of late August air, tangy as the blue sky above them. As she stood on the porch waiting for Gavi, Pleasant Plains stretched before her, spreading from the sandy riverbank to the ever-receding line of trees. The town seemed to sprout a new building each month. The Lightcap's Livery Stable had come first, then a newspaper office next door to Stuart Keith's law offices, and a cobbler's shop to supply a saddle now and then. A courthouse had been built on the new town square, and trees had been planted. The town had even hauled one of the cannons that over-looked the river into the center of the square where small boys sat astride it, firing imaginary rounds at pirates, British troops, or Indians.

Millie turned away from the town toward the Kankakee marsh. The edges of the marsh came very close to the foot of Keith Hill, following a stream that flowed into the river, but the marsh proper, a hundred miles of untamed wilder-ness, was hidden now by a mist drawn up by the morning sun. *Here there be monsters.* Millie shivered with delight. *This* was what she had missed while she was in the South—the wildness and freedom of space and thought.

Millie knew that God was with her always, but some-how she felt closer to Him when she walked and talked with Him along the paths of the marsh. She loved the thought that He designed the petals of the tiniest flowers. He had set the jewels in the dragonfly's eyes. He knew everything that happened in the dark, secret nest of the muskrat.

"Your mother thought we might want to go into town and visit with Helen and Claudina," Gavi said, coming out the door.

"That might be fun . . ."

"But?"

"I have been longing for a ramble in the marsh since I came home."

# Millie's Great Adventure

"Isn't it dangerous?" Gavi asked. "Couldn't there be Indians or wild beasts?"

"The Indians have all been driven out by the government," Millie said. "And that is a pity. The tribe we met when we moved here were very nice people. As for wild beasts . . . this is the frontier, after all. We will simply have to keep our wits about us."

"Then the marsh it is," Gavi said, "if you want company."

"Do you have walking shoes?"

"I am wearing them," Gavi said, lifting her skirts to show the boots. "But I might want a different bonnet."

Millie found her sturdy brogans under the bed where she had left them a year before. She quickly pulled them on, and put her sketchpad and charcoal into the satchel she had used for a hundred such expeditions. She chose a wide-brimmed bonnet, tied it under her chin with a ribbon, and picked up a parasol.

"You are the perfect picture of an explorer," Gavi laughed when they met on the porch once more. "In every particular, save for the parasol."

"I *am* an explorer," Millie said, lifting her chin. "And one never knows when one might need a parasol. Aunt Wealthy doesn't leave home without hers, and she is the most adventuresome of women."

Bobforshort followed them down the path to the edge of the garden, then whined.

"Cyril is reading his lessons," Millie told the dog. "And so is Fan."

It was fortunate for the hound that Fan and Cyril spent most of their time together, for it tore his hound heart apart to leave one and follow the other. Realizing that neither was along for this expedition, he went back to the porch to wait patiently for lessons and chores to be over.

Millie was just as glad to leave him. She liked walking quietly, watching for small creatures, and they were never seen when Bob galloped along. She linked arms with Gavi as they walked down Keith Hill to the wooden bridge.

"The Kankakee is like no other place on earth," Millie said, "wonderful and wild. I have been longing for it ever since we arrived. Look!" A Cooper's Hawk brushed the morning sky with its wings. "Mr. Audubon did a marvelous drawing of Cooper's Hawks. I'll show you when we get home. Aunt Wealthy sent me books about birds during the year that I was so ill, because I could watch them from the parlor window."

"I can't imagine you as a bundled invalid on a parlor couch," Gavriel said. "You have roses in your cheeks and stars in your eyes." She stopped. "Did you hear something?"

Millie untied her bonnet and pulled it off so she could listen. There was *something* moving through the underbrush. She held her finger to her lips, a sign for Gavi to remain silent. The sounds drew near, and the hair on Millie's neck prickled.

*Is it following us? Gordon told me of people who disappeared into the Kankakee without a trace.* "Walk carefully, Millie Keith," he had said one day when she exclaimed over the beauty of the flowers. "The marsh is beautiful, but wild. There is death here for those who do not respect it."

Suddenly a huge tom turkey strutted onto the path. He fixed the girls with one startled beady eye, as surprised to see them as they were to see him. Then he disappeared back into the bushes.

A nervous laugh exploded from Gavi. "I thought we were being stalked by something the size of a rhinoceros," she said. "How could one bird make so much noise? I'm afraid I am a city girl, Millie, and out of my element here."

"So was I," Millie said, glad she had managed not to scream when the turkey appeared, "until my illness. Gordon would sit with me when he could, telling me about the birds and small animals. On good days he would take me walking in the marsh. He knows as much about the birds and small creatures as Mr. Audubon, I'm sure, but his art is not with pens and ink. Gordon was a carver before his terrible accident. You've seen the angel that stands guard over our family Bible?"

"It's beautiful," Gavi said.

"Gordon carved it before his accident." Millie went on to describe the musket accident that had shot a ramrod through Gordon's hand and into his chest, crippling his hand and stealing his future as a carver.

"He's been a good friend to you and your family," Gavi said. "Has your heart never gone toward him?"

"I have always thought of Gordon as a brother," Millie said. "And he has always treated me as a sister." She released Gavi's arm and jumped a small stream. Gavi followed, and Millie ducked under a branch, searching until she found a faint game trail leading into the tangle of mayapples and hazel bushes.

"Gordon is as at home in the Kankakee as other people are in a sitting room," Millie said, holding a branch aside so Gavi could follow. "I've seen him sit so still that wild deer eat from his hands. They won't come near me."

"The Lightcaps are not at all like any family I have ever met," Gavi observed. "They are . . ." she looked to the clouds, as if she were searching for words there, " . . . out of place. Almost like creatures from a fairy tale. Rhoda Jane would be the princess, and Gordon . . ." she shrugged. "How on earth did they come to Pleasant Plains?"

"Why, they stepped right out of Shakespeare," Millie said with a laugh. "Mr. Lightcap was an actor. When he couldn't support his growing family on the stage, he would turn to the trade he had learned from his father — smithing. He stopped in Pleasant Plains to make a little money for the road. The ague was bad that year. Mr. Lightcap lingered for a month."

"If you were me, would you allow Gordon to go?" Gavi asked suddenly, and then before Millie could open her mouth, she added, "Don't answer that. I know it's something I have to decide myself. I just keep thinking, what kind of young man would leave his family, leave his business, to help someone he hardly knows? Someone he will never see again, if he is successful."

*Was there a catch in Gavi's voice?* Millie glanced at her, but Gavi turned away.

They walked for a long time in silence, finally reaching a brushy tussock. Gavi suggested a rest, and Millie agreed, settling herself on a rock with her pad and charcoal. Gavi went a little farther down the hill and sat with her own thoughts.

It wasn't an uncomfortable silence. The wildness was big enough for them to be alone, even though they could see each other, and they kept each other company in the silence.

Flipping through the pages of her sketchbook, Millie started with the crude sketches she had drawn after Aunt Wealthy had sent her the bird books. She stopped at the picture of the muskrat she had attempted on her last visit to the Kankakee, before traveling to her Uncle Horace's plantation.

# Millie's Great Adventure

She had to laugh at her sketch of the creature. Gordon had corrected her drawing, making it identifiable, with a few brief lines. When she'd asked him how he did that, he said he just drew the muskrat God intended . . . and she'd known what he meant right away. Only God could make the muskrat, but Gordon's lines were enough like it to remind her of what God had done.

The next page held her ridiculous profile of her Uncle Horace, which had been skewed when the stage hit a rock. Millie's soul ached as she traced the potato-shaped lump that was supposed to have been his nose. *Uncle Horace is not what God intended him to be. Not yet. How could he be when he isn't a Christian?* Still, she could see flashes of what God intended in her uncle's concern for others and his sense of humor.

Millie's heart ached as she turned the pages, remembering her time at Roselands. Aunt Isabel, as vain and selfish as Jezebel of old; the Dinsmore children, rich in every worldly way, yet starving for the love and attention Isabel lavished only on herself; Laylie, the little slave girl whose courage had captured Millie's heart and challenged her faith. Millie turned past the quick study of Laylie. She had hoped to bring Laylie to Pleasant Plains as a sister, but God had other plans, and now she was sure they would not meet again this side of heaven.

Peach blossoms. The page-turning slowed again. Spring at Roselands when she admitted that she was in love with Charles Landreth. A pelican on the deck of a ship. That had made her laugh. The absurd creature had been a ship's pet on a boat she had taken to Viamede, the plantation of little Elsie Dinsmore, Cousin Horace's daughter. How was little Elsie faring at Roselands? Millie still prayed for her every morning and night.

# Wise Counsel

And now Millie was home again, in the Kankakee, with a fresh, clean page before her and no idea what her future held. *Charles . . .*

*That's enough of that!* Millie told herself briskly. *I have turned past those pages and have a new one before me.* She decided to sketch the tree that clung to the side of the hill. She drew a few quick lines, then held it up. Not bad at all. Only . . . if she turned it sideways and added a tail just so, and a fang or two, it would be a perfect sea serpent. *Here there be . . .*

"Either my stomach is growling, or there is something fierce in the bushes."

Millie jumped at the sound of Gavi's voice. "I suppose it is time to start home," Millie said, squinting at the sun. "Mamma was wonderful to let us come, but I'm sure she could use some help with dinner." She packed up her drawing supplies and opened her pink parasol against the sun. "Ready?"

Millie had learned long ago that the marsh could be deceptive, so they followed their own footprints down the trail. They stopped where two game paths crossed and examined the ground. Their own boot marks showed clearly which way they had come, but Gavi pointed at a mark on the other trail. "That's no turkey track," she said.

Millie knelt and touched the pug mark. "It might be a bear," she said. "I've never seen one in the Kankakee. I believe they prefer the forest to the wetlands, but I can't think of anything else that large." Gavi looked around uneasily. "Don't worry," Millie said, "it's an old print. See how the edges here are crumbled? Whatever made it is long gone." She unpacked her sketchpad and, measuring with her hands, marked the edges of the print, then traced the shape onto her paper.

"Gordon will know for sure," Millie said, "or Celestia Ann."

"The preacher's wife?"

"She knows more about the Kankakee than any of us," Millie said. "She grew up on the edge of the marsh."

"I was thinking of visiting them, actually," Gavi said. "I want . . . I need prayers for wisdom. I want to make the right decision for Jed and Jaz, as well as for myself."

"Why not now?" Millie asked. "It's not far, if we skirt the bottom of Keith Hill. And I can ask her about the print."

They found Reverend Matthew Lord in the front yard, watching over his tiny wife. Millie still could not help but smile at the couple. They seemed as mismatched as any two people could possibly be. Matthew Lord was tall, angular, and thin, with arms too long for his jacket sleeves and pants perpetually too short for his long legs—until his Celestia Ann had taken over the care of his wardrobe.

When she first met Reverend Lord, Millie's impression had been that Ichabod Crane had somehow walked right out of the pages of *The Legend of Sleepy Hollow*. To Millie's relief, Matthew Lord's exterior was deceptive. If people's outsides had looked like their insides, she was sure he would look like a mix of King David, Solomon, and perhaps a dash of Jeremiah just for good measure. The young reverend had a passion for God's Word and for caring for His people. He had been educated in the finest schools in the East, and he loved reading and discussing history and philosophy with Stuart Keith.

No one would have imagined Reverend Lord and Celestia Ann as man and wife—no one but God. If angels wore calico, then Millie was sure they would look just as tiny Celestia Ann did now, with her wild red hair a halo over her sweet face. She'd made quite a different picture the first time Millie had seen her standing on the Keiths' doorstep. She'd been wearing men's overalls rather than pantalets under her thin cotton dress, and her uncombable hair was stuffed under a fedora. Again, looks had been deceiving. Celestia Ann was nothing less than Queen Esther before the beauty treatments. It required only soap, a comb, and a little love to let what was inside shine out to the world.

With Celestia Ann's care, her young husband's cuffs were always the right length, and his coat, if threadbare, was always clean and brushed. She, in turn, had bloomed into one of the leading ladies of the church, respected and loved by all.

"Let me do that, dear. I'm sure you shouldn't be gardening," Matthew was saying as the girls walked up.

"Don't worry so much, Matthew," Celestia Ann said, straightening. "The baby's not due for weeks, and work never hurt me before. Why, hello there, Millie, Gavi."

"Good day, ladies!" Reverend Lord said. "Have you been walking? It's a marvelous day for exercise."

"Yes, it is, and yes, we were," Millie said, taking out her sketchpad. "We saw a print on the trail." She flipped open the pad.

Celestia Ann squinted at Millie's drawing. "That's either a couple of pigs or a bear print. Black bears come down to the marsh sometimes."

Millie turned her pad upside down. "It doesn't look at all like pigs!"

"I can see them," Gavi said, pointing. "That would be an ear, and—"

"It's a bear print," Millie said, shutting the pad.

# Millie's Great Adventure

"The *ursus americanus* is normally shy," Matthew Lord said, then blushed. "According to my books."

"They're pretty good eating, too," Celestia Ann added. Gavi and Millie glanced at each other, trying not to laugh. If confronted with a bear, the first thing that Matthew Lord would think of was his natural science books; the first thing Celestia Ann thought of would be how to cook it.

Matthew took both his wife's hands in his and looked into her eyes. "Dear," he said seriously, "I want you to promise me that you will not go hunting bears. I have read that they can be very dangerous."

"I won't go hunting bears," she said, looking at him earnestly, "anymore."

"Anymore?" His Adam's apple bobbed.

"I suppose you don't want me to bring my bearskin rug from Mother's house either," she said. "But it was a good shot, and I'm proud of that rug. I can just see little Matthew crawling around on it."

"On a dead bear?"

"I think Matthew David Crockett Lord would like a dead bear," Celestia Ann said with a twinkle in her eye.

"David *Crockett*?"

"A frontier baby needs a frontier name," Celestia Ann said. "My daddy is good friends with Mr. Crockett."

"I think that Matthew would rather enjoy live bears at a distance," Matthew said.

"I was wondering if I could talk to you both," Gavi said. "I think I need prayer."

For the next hour, Millie listened as Gavi told her story once again.

"Let Gordon find him," Celestia Ann said, as if anyone could see the sense of it. "You never know why Rayme didn't show up. He could be in trouble of some kind."

"You don't think it improper of Gordon to offer?"

"There is not an improper bone in Gordon Lightcap's body," Reverend Lord said. "He is a fine and godly young man."

"Thank you," Gavi said, rising from her seat. "We need to get home, Millie."

Fan was sitting on the porch with her arms around Bob when they arrived. "Millie, do you think anyone would buy Bob?" she asked. " 'Cause I think Mamma wants to sell him."

"Why would she want to do that?" Millie asked.

"Bob carried a baby chipmunk into the house."

"Surely Mamma would just put it outside."

"That's what I thought," Fan said, "but it started running around, and Mamma tried to hit it with a broom and she knocked over her blue china vase."

The blue china vase was Marcia's favorite, carried carefully all the way from Lansdale, Ohio.

"Do you think Mamma will sell him?" Fan asked again.

"I think perhaps you should take him on a little walk," Millie said.

Marcia was sweeping up the remains of the vase when they went in.

"Don't throw it away," Gavi said. "I believe I can mend it." She prepared a glue from milk, egg whites, and powdered lime, and set about piecing the vase together.

"How did you learn to mend china?" Marcia asked.

"Gordon taught me," Gavi said, "when a gravy bowl broke."

"Oh, yes." Marcia shook her head. "Gordon can fix anything." She put away her broom and went back to dinner preparation.

# Millie's Great Adventure

"I think I will accept Gordon's offer," Gavi said, looking up from her work. "It would be better for all of us if . . ."

"If?" Millie prompted.

"If he finds Rayme quickly."

# CHAPTER 3

# Losses and Gains

*But whatever was to my profit I now*
*consider loss for the sake of Christ.*
*What is more, I consider everything*
*a loss compared to the surpassing*
*greatness of knowing Christ*
*Jesus my Lord, for whose sake*
*I have lost all things.*

PHILIPPIANSS 3:7–8

# Losses and Gains

*M*illie adjusted her periwinkle cap and smiled approvingly at her reflection in the glass of the china cabinet. "So, Miss Keith," she said, speaking sternly to the image of the pert young lady in a simply cut gown with a jaunty hat, "you want to be an explorer and naturalist by day and dance until dawn each night?" Her reflection did not look a bit dismayed by the dichotomy. Millie thought there was nothing wrong with wishing for a perfect world—full of adventure, lace doilies, and tea cakes. The few opportunities to dress up in Pleasant Plains left the young ladies with a desire for the feel of silk, satin, and the rustle of lace.

Millie adjusted her cap to a more jaunty angle. Claudina Chetwood was hosting the weekly Bible study, and she had made an occasion of it, sending formal invitations to a Bible Study and High Tea. Millie, Gavi, and Zillah were about to depart.

"I am still not certain I want to go, Millie," Gavi said, coming into the parlor. "I feel like a . . . a spectacle."

"Well, you look like a vision," Millie assured her. "If your grandmother chose that dress, she had excellent taste in style and color."

"It's not my wardrobe that worries me," Gavi said. Gordon had been putting the stables in order for his absence. It was agreed that Gavi would move to the station to help Rhoda Jane run the stables while he was away, with Stuart Keith and Matthew Lord helping with the heavy work when necessary. Gavi blushed. "By now everyone in town knows that I have a missing husband."

# Millie's Great Adventure

"That's true," Millie said, picking up her reticule and Bible. "News seems to seep through walls here, no matter how circumspect you try to be. But you can't hide yourself away until Gordon finds him."

"I think it's terribly romantic," Zillah said. "Perhaps Rayme has taken a fall—eeek!" She gave a demonstration of the possibility by tripping over the corner of the carpet and lunging toward Millie.

Millie caught her arm. "Glide, Zillah, glide!"

"Gliding isn't working."

"Try walking tippy-toe." Had it been only a year ago that she had learned herself? Millie smiled as she watched her sister, her heels not even touching the ground. "That's a little better," she said. Marcia had given Zillah permission to borrow Millie's button boots only after Zillah had pointed out that her church shoes no longer fit, and the dress was just short enough to show her ugly brogans peeking out beneath.

"Heels make all the difference," Zillah said. "I feel positively *elegant*!" She tottered elegantly to the couch to prove it and settled onto the cushions. "My point was, Rayme might have amnesia!"

Millie sighed. Zillah had borrowed several romance novels from Lu Grange. Her imagination had been completely captured by the romantically missing Rayme Romanik.

"Does Sheriff Ormsby ever attend the Bible study?" Zillah asked, folding her little ladylike hands in her lap.

*Almost completely captured*, Millie corrected herself. "Wallace rarely attends the young ladies' group. Are we ready to go?"

Zillah gathered up her things and they said good-bye to Marcia, Adah, Fan, Celestia Ann, and the little girls in the kitchen.

"You all look lovely," Marcia said. "I'm sure you will have a wonderful time. Do you have the list of dry goods, Millie?"

Millie assured her the list was in her reticule.

"Don't eat too many tea cakes," Celestia Ann added. "Or you won't have any room for the doughnuts we're making!"

"Yeah, Millie," Fan said. "I want you to eat some of my doughnuts! You too, Gavi."

Millie assured her sister that they would save room for at least one doughnut. At the gate she stopped to open her parasol.

"Hey, Millie." Don came out of the hydrangea bushes and pulled the gate open for her. Cyril and Jed were peering over his shoulder. "May we walk to town with you?"

"We'll carry your Bibles," Jed offered.

"And help you bring home the things Mamma wants from the Mercantile," said Don.

"And keep Zillah from fallin' off of them stilts." Cyril offered his arm.

"What are you up to, Jedidiah?" Gavi asked.

"Marbles," Jed said, pulling three marbles—two porcelain, one wooden—from his pocket.

Cyril elbowed him, and he put the marbles away. "Mamma said to get out from under foot."

"She said to make ourselves useful," Don corrected. "We thought we'd make ourselves useful by escorting you ladies." He bowed.

"And?" Millie prompted.

"John Geasly is in town," Don said. "He comes on his uncle's barge on Wednesdays. He's been winnin' all the marbles in Pleasant Plains."

"Prob'ly all the marbles clear to Chicago," Jed said. "But Don can beat him. Don has a genuine Indian-made shooter."

"Are you sure Ru isn't painting the barn this afternoon?" Millie asked suspiciously.

"Honest, Millie," Don said, "Ru is digging in the garden, and he likes to do that alone. Mamma and Celestia Ann are talking about *babies*." The boys all nodded. "She said we could go with you if you needed any help."

"I do believe I will have several packages to carry home," Millie said graciously.

"You're the best, Millie," Cyril said. "If you ever need anything, anything at all, you just ask Don."

"Hey!" His twin punched his arm. Bobforshort loped after Cyril, keeping his tail down as long as Fan might see him from the window. As soon as they were out of sight, he perked up and chased a gray squirrel and two rabbits.

Don offered Zillah his arm when she had to walk over rough ground along the path, or through the sand in the streets of Pleasant Plains. Zillah would no doubt have been able to walk very well, if she hadn't been trying to catch glimpses of herself in shop windows.

Wallace Ormsby himself stepped out of the law office he shared with Mr. Keith. Zillah stopped dead in her tracks as he walked toward them.

"Good day, ladies," Wallace said, tipping his hat, "and gentlemen." It took a full minute to animate Zillah once more, and then Cyril had to lead her around a watering trough she almost tumbled into.

At the Chetwoods' door, the boys said good-bye. "We'll meet you at the Mercantile," Don said, bouncing in anticipation.

"Bible study's a good thing," Cyril said. "Take as long as you want!"

Gavi had been very quiet on the walk to town. Now she threw one panicked glance to Millie as the door opened.

"Gavi!" Claudina cried, drawing her inside, "I'm so glad you have come!"

Claudina seated Gavriel beside sweet Effie Prescott, who gave her a shy smile. Millie sat beside Damaris.

Millie looked around the faces gathered in the room — Lu, Helen, Claudina, Rhoda Jane — and her heart sent up a silent prayer of thanks. For all their differences, Millie could see one thing in the faces of the girls: Jesus. His Spirit had come ahead of them, making a way for Gavi.

When the meeting was over, Gavi and Millie walked toward the Mercantile. "I did enjoy the meeting," Gavi said. "It reminded me of Granmarie, of home." They stepped from the sandy street up onto the boardwalk in front of Monocker's Mercantile to see the boys, who had been shooting marbles. "Why, Don, what's wrong?"

Don was leaning against the wall, his hands shoved deep in his pockets. His freckles stood out like pepper on his salt-white face. Cyril and Jed looked equally distressed. Even Bob half-drooped off the boardwalk where he lay, his ears hanging in the dust.

"It's his shooter," Cyril said, putting his arm around Don's shoulders. "John took it, and there's no way Don's gonna win it back. Not ever."

"Yeah," Jed said, "cause John won't give him the chance."

"That was the best marble in town, next to my stone beauty."

"It was better," Don said, shaking his head.

"I'm very sorry for your loss," Millie said. "But perhaps you should not have played keeps with it."

"Aw, Millie." Don pushed himself away from the door. "Girls just don't understand marbles. What good would having an Indian shooter be unless I used it?"

43

Millie led the way into the Mercantile, leaving the boys in a dejected huddle on the hitching post.

"Is there any mail for the Keiths?" she asked.

"Nothing." Mrs. Monocker pursed her lips. "What is wrong with that young man of yours?"

Millie turned pink to her fingertips. *What is wrong with Charles? Surely my last letter reached him, and he's had time to respond. Is he still reading the Bible? Could he have forgotten me so soon?* Millie felt tears start to well, and turned quickly to examine a bolt of cloth as she blinked them away.

"Did Marcia send a list, dear?" Mrs. Monocker asked kindly.

Millie handed her the list and retreated to the privacy afforded by a pile of potato bags. Gavi pretended fascination with the onion bins while Millie dabbed her eyes.

"Hey!" Cyril had followed them into the store. "Why's Millie cryin'?"

"It's that young man," Mrs. Monocker whispered loudly. "He's broken her heart."

"He certainly has not," Millie said, gathering her packages. "My heart is fine. Just fine!"

"Of course it is, dear." Mrs. Monocker gave her a knowing look. "Fine as thistledown and right as rain. Why don't you have a nice peppermint stick?"

The boys' feet dragged as they carried the packages home. Gavi was lost in her own thoughts, and Millie's mind kept turning to Charles. Even Bob moped along until they reached the foot of the hill. Suddenly the memory of Fan waiting for him percolated up from the depths of his brain. He bayed his special bellow and raced ahead of them up the hill. He was wagging his stub of a tail and eating doughnut holes when they arrived.

"Why the long faces?" Marcia asked when they came in. Jed told her about the marble. "That's too bad, Don. Perhaps this will cheer you up," she said, placing a plate of fresh doughnuts on the table. "And if that's not enough, a parcel arrived while you were gone. A box from Aunt Wealthy. She sent it along with a stage driver, and Gordon dropped it off not an hour ago." A package from Aunt Wealthy meant books, and that was enough to cheer even Don. "We will open it after supper. You boys go help Ru with the afternoon chores. I think he will be able to find plenty for you to do."

Millie took over the preparation of supper, while Zillah told Adah all about the Bible study, and Gavi took Annis and Jaz to play in the yard.

After supper Stuart read from the big Family Bible, one complete chapter as he did each and every night. Marcia led the family in only one hymn instead of two, as the boys were having a hard time paying attention with the box from Aunt Wealthy sitting in the corner. Finally Stuart called for a knife, the twine was cut, the brown paper removed, and the box lid opened.

Aunt Wealthy had included a paper of pins for Zillah, India rubber balls and wooden tops for the boys, a moccasin pattern for Fan (which she claimed to have gotten from a missionary to the Mohicans), and a new pen-and-ink set for Adah.

"Have you been writing her often enough?" Marcia asked.

"I suppose not," Adah admitted.

Next was a set of colored inks for Ru's plans and a drawing pad for Millie. Finally Stuart pulled out five thick books, and the wonderful new-book-smell of leather and ink filled the room.

# Millie's Great Adventure

"What books are they?" Fan asked.

The titles were in French and Millie translated: "*The Adventures of the Swiss Family Robinson*, in five volumes. By a lady author named Madame de Montholieu. No, Madame de Montholieu is the translator.*" She opened the first book and a folded note fell out.

"My dearest ones," Millie spoke what Aunt Wealthy had written. "Although you are living on the wild frontier, I am sure Marcia has not neglected your education. I am confident in sending these books, knowing that you will enjoy them, and they will increase your knowledge of a lovely language. I enjoyed them greatly myself, although there are certain errors in the portrayal of flora and fauna. The Swiss pastor who wrote the story was not well traveled, I presume. Love, Aunt Wealthy."

It was true that Marcia had insisted her children learn French along with their arithmetic and history. Millie's grasp of the language was better than it had been when they had first moved to Pleasant Plains and she had used it to speak with the Potawatami Indians. Wealthy had once preached a sermon from the Keiths' front porch in French.

"Reading this story is an excellent idea," Stuart said. "Though you might have to take over the reading, dear. My French could use improvement."

"Will you start it tonight, Mamma?" Adah asked.

"Not everyone here knows French," Marcia pointed out.

"Don't let that stop you, please," Gavi said. "Jed and I do understand a little, as many of our Romani friends speak French. We might even learn a word or two."

Annis and Jaz were already nodding sleepily, so Marcia set aside her needle and took up a book. The Keiths' parlor was unusually quiet as everyone sat listening. The little girls fell asleep, but Fan interrupted frequently, asking about words she did not understand, until Millie pulled her little sister onto her lap so that she could whisper the explanations in her ear.

Marcia's beautiful voice soon drew them all into the story of a Christian family on a ship in a terrible storm. They escaped death only to find themselves on a deserted island where they had to hunt for food and shelter. They did not read many pages, as Marcia often stopped to explain unfamiliar words, but the story was exciting and full of action. By the time she set the book aside, even Cyril was sitting at her feet.

"Well now!" Stuart said, "How *does* Aunt Wealthy know these things?"

"I believe we have a mutual Friend who whispers secrets to Aunt Wealthy," Marcia laughed. "I can think of no other explanation."

"What things, Pappa?" Adah asked. "What secret does Aunt Wealthy know?"

"Why, that we are going to have our very own adventure," Stuart said.

"What do you mean?" Zillah asked, a little alarmed. "I don't want to leave Pleasant Plains!"

"We won't have to leave home, dear," Marcia said. "Sometimes you find an adventure, and sometimes an adventure finds you. The storm in the book blew the Robinsons' ship onto rocks. We had a storm that blew our garden away, and our henhouse as well."

"That adventure's over," Don said.

"Not quite." Stuart shook his head. "You may have realized that my law practice is not going as well as we had hoped this summer."

# Millie's Great Adventure

Millie's heart sank. She had known the egg and butter money was gone from the jar above the stove, and there had been no money to buy Fan new boots, but she had somehow thought that it would all work out when her parents returned. Now as she looked around at the faces of her brothers and sisters, she could not help thinking that it was her fault. Stuart's practice had not done well because he had not been home. He had traveled hundreds of miles over two months to bring Millie home, and then spent another month in Lansdale with Aunt Wealthy.

As if seeing her thoughts, Stuart went on. "Things have not been going well for many people in Pleasant Plains, as a matter of fact. No one has the money to pay for a lawyer just now, and that means the Keiths are short on funds to make it through the winter."

"What does that mean, Pappa?" Adah asked.

"Are we going to starve to death?" Fan asked.

"Of course not!" Marcia said.

"Of course not," Stuart echoed. "Don't you remember Jesus' words? 'So do not worry about what you will eat, or what you will wear. Your heavenly Father knows that you need them. But seek first his kingdom, and all things will be added unto you.' I can't seek His Kingdom by demanding our neighbors pay money they do not have."

"We always seek His Kingdom, Pappa," Zillah pointed out. "But you just said that we have no money!"

" 'All things' means everything you need," Marcia explained. "Not everything you want. This winter will be a great adventure in trusting God."

"Like the Robinsons," Ru said, and Marcia nodded.

"It is going to require some ingenuity," Stuart said, "and some sacrifice."

"Like in the Bible?" Fan asked. "Are we going to put something on the altar and burn it up?"

"Not exactly," Stuart said. "In this case sacrifice means we are going to have to give up some things that we are used to having. The twister didn't touch the hay field, and we can mow. Belle will have plenty of hay, but we will have to sell the horses. I have already talked to a family named Jones in the next town who want to buy Glory and Esther. They have two little boys who will take very good care of them."

"Pappa!" Fan cried. "Not Glory! Gavi's going to help me teach her tricks!"

"Fan, dear," Marcia said gently, "you wouldn't want Glory to be hungry, would you?"

Fan shook her golden curls.

"And if we couldn't feed her, she would be very, very hungry."

Annis's lower lip quivered. "Are we going to be very hungry, Mamma?"

"Not if we work hard," Stuart said. "People have been living in Indiana for a very long time without chickens and eggs or even gardens."

"We didn't have those things when we came here," Zillah said. "We bought food at the Mercantile. Can't we do that again, Pappa?"

"We had a small amount of money set aside for our move. We have almost none left. We could run a bill at the store, but I would rather not be in debt."

"Were you talking about Indians, Pappa?" Ru was on the edge of his seat. "I read a great deal about the lives of the Potawatami before we came. They lived off the land, hunting and fishing and gathering berries and nuts."

Cyril's ears perked up. "Don and me can fish," he said. "And hunt, too, if we had a gun."

"Don and I," Millie corrected.

"I don't like fish," Fan said, wrinkling her nose.

"You will like it better than being hungry," Adah pointed out.

"The best fishin' hours are in the morning," Cyril said. "Too bad that's when we're sittin' here with books and slates."

"I was thinking the same thing," Stuart said with a twinkle in his eye. "Too bad you are going to miss lessons for a time, but it can't be helped."

"Stuart!" Marcia said. "It's bad enough that there is no boys' school in Pleasant Plains. I hardly think that we can let the boys skip their morning lessons for months at a time!"

"There will be plenty of time after it snows to catch up," he said. "And I will give the boys lessons myself. They will be studying French every night as we read, as well."

"You mean . . ." Cyril stood up slowly, as if his father's words were too wonderful to comprehend. "You mean no more morning lessons until it *snows*?"

"That's what I mean," Stuart said. "It won't do you much good to have perfect spelling scores if you have nothing in your stomach in December."

"Thank You, God!" Cyril cried, throwing his arms into the air.

CHAPTER

4

# Many Hands Make Light Work

*God is not unjust; he will not forget your work and the love you have shown him as you have helped his people and continue to help them. . . . We do not want you to become lazy, but to imitate those who through faith and patience inherit what has been promised.*

HEBREWS 6:10, 12

On the eve of Gordon's departure, the Keiths, Lightcaps, and Lords met for prayer. Gordon talked for two hours with Gavi, getting as much information as possible about Rayme Romanik and the people he might know, the places he had been.

Although they sat far apart and the tone of their conversation was proper and abrupt, by the end of the evening Millie was quite sure that Gavi was right. It would be better for everyone if Gordon found Rayme quickly.

The next morning Gordon arrived with a wagon to carry Gavi, Jed, and Jaz, as well as their trunks, down to the stage station. Marcia and the Keith girls were helped into the wagon as well, finding seats atop the trunks, with Stuart and the boys walking alongside as Gordon drove. Mrs. Lightcap was sweeping the station porch when they arrived. She beamed at Gavi as Gordon lifted the young woman from the wagon.

"Gordon," she said happily, "you didn't tell me you were married! And grandchildren, too." She beamed at Jaz and Jed. "Isn't that nice!"

"Gordon's not married, Mother," Rhoda Jane said gently. "This is Gavriel, remember? You met her at church."

"Yes, Gavriel," Mrs. Lightcap said. "I remember the wedding. There was a big yellow butterfly."

"Was there a butterfly at your wedding, Mother?" Rhoda Jane suggested. "Perhaps that is what you are remembering."

"No, it was Gordon's wedding," she insisted, then she put her hand to her head. "Only it couldn't have been. It was Jesus' butterfly; He sent it . . ."

Emmaretta took her mother's hand and pulled her away, and Gordon and Ru carried the trunks inside. The stage rolled in just as they carried the last trunk up the steps, and Gavriel set about changing the teams in her no-nonsense way. The driver stood chewing a straw while Gavi led the tired team away to be watered, fed, and rubbed down.

"Lady stable hand," he remarked when the work was done. "Don't that beat all. Are we ready to go?"

Gordon appeared with his carpetbag, ready to leave. He shook Stuart's hand, then hugged and kissed Emmaretta and Min and his mother.

"Don't forget the cream," Mrs. Lightcap said, handing him a shopping list. "I can't frost a cake without it!"

"I won't forget it, Mother." He turned to Rhoda Jane. "You are sure that you will be able to—"

"I'm sure," Rhoda Jane said, linking arms with Gavi. "I have plenty of help, and if we need more, we will call Millie."

"Well, that's all right then," Gordon said with a laugh. "I'm sure the three of you could take over the world."

"Mrs. Romanik." He appeared to be speaking to a sign over Gavi's head. "I'll find him. I promise."

"Thank you," Gavi said to the dust at Gordon's feet.

The driver gave a final call, and Gordon boarded the stage.

<hr />

"I like that young man," Stuart said as they walked home.

"I do, too," Marcia said, taking his hand.

"I want to hold Pappa's hand!" Annis tried to wiggle in between her parents.

"You may hold my right hand," Stuart said. "The left is closest to my heart, and that one belongs to your Mamma."

Fan had to settle for Millie's hand.

"Do you think Gordon will ever get married, Pappa?" Zillah asked.

Millie sighed. She had thought she was the only one who saw the hurt in Gordon's eyes.

"I expect he will," Stuart said. "If one of my daughters finds a young man like that, I would not be opposed."

"I'll take Gordon," Fan said with a skip. "I like him."

Stuart pursed his lips. "Hmmmm. If he's available when you are thirty-five, we will talk."

"Thirty-five! Pappa!" Zillah wailed. "That's far too old for marriage!"

"Oh, don't worry," Don said. "Wallace will only be forty-two when you are thirty-five."

"What's this?" Stuart said, raising his eyebrows. "Wallace Ormsby?"

"It's nothing," Zillah said, glaring at her brother.

"Zillah's gonna throw me in the swamp if I tell you she's in love with Wallace," Fan declared.

"And the bugsies and beasties will eat her," Annis said, nodding solemnly.

Zillah's face was three shades beyond scarlet.

"No one will be thrown in the swamp," Marcia said firmly. "And no one will be getting married anytime soon, either. So I suggest we get back to the business at hand. Had you planned to bake today, Millie? I think Mrs. Simon might like a loaf of fresh bread."

# Millie's Great Adventure

With the Mikolauses moved to the stage station, the Keiths settled down to the serious business of preparing for winter. The first concern was keeping warm. Last year they had paid a man from town to haul the wood they would need for the fireplaces and the cookstove. This year Stuart and Ru would have to cut the wood themselves. Stuart exchanged his suit for trousers and suspenders, and his pen and law books for a crosscut saw and ax. Glory, the sturdier of the mares, was enlisted to snake the trees from the woods and pull them up the hill. Then the trees were cut into lengths, and Don and Cyril set to splitting the wood and stacking it. As Millie watched how slowly the woodpile grew, she prayed for Indian summer, that long warm spell in autumn, to give them more time.

Millie helped her mother take inventory of the kitchen sup- plies—one barrel of flour, already half gone; tomatoes that had been canned the summer before, gathering dust in the corners of the shelves; and salt. Everything above ground in Ru's garden had been destroyed by the hail in the tornado, but onions, potatoes, and carrots were still harvestable.

"I think we need to get the berries from the marsh," Marcia said one morning. "The potatoes and carrots will wait, but the berries will not. I think we should all go berry- picking this morning!"

"You will come with us?" Millie asked in surprise. "I'm so glad!" Millie gathered buckets and inspected her sisters' bonnets and shoes to make sure everyone was prepared for tromping through wetlands. She picked up her parasol and led the way. She didn't want to take the girls too far into the marsh, so she led them to bushes along the edges. They filled their pails well before noon, then sat down to a picnic of bread and cheese.

# Many Hands Make Light Work

"I see why you love it here, Millie," Marcia said, leaning back so the sun shined on her face. Millie felt a sudden wave of sadness. Marcia would have loved the walks, the fresh air and exercise. But the weight of the household, which Millie had carried for six weeks, was hers every day. Time for herself was a luxury Marcia Keith had left behind when she followed her husband onto the frontier. Gowns and balls, concerts and long walks in her own garden . . . *Could Fan even remember when Mamma was one of the leading ladies in the society of Lansdale, Ohio? When Mamma went to concerts in the evening with Pappa, and held balls at their fine home, and hired servants to do the washing and cooking? Annis was too young to remember, of course. Zillah was just old enough to remember and to wish for times long past.*

"I can't help but think," Marcia said, "how good God is."

"Yes, Mamma," Millie said, swallowing hard.

"And now it's time to get back to work."

They carried their buckets home.

"Leave that dog on the porch," Marcia said as they reached the door. Bob had found a lovely mess of mud, and even the walk home through the tall grasses had not cleaned his feet and legs. Fan pressed him into a sitting position on the boards of the porch and told him to stay as they all took off their muddy shoes and went inside in their stocking feet to deposit the berries in the kitchen.

"Mamma, I was wondering if—" Ru stopped in midsentence as Bob pushed past him, racing in all his muddy glory up the stairs after Fan. Ru ran after him and finally hauled the dog from under Fan's bed, leaving a trail of mud and leaves as he dragged him back to the door.

Fan was set to sweeping up the mess as Millie cleaned the mud from their shoes. By the time she was finished, Marcia was already boiling jars for canning.

57

# Millie's Great Adventure

"Say," Cyril said, taking a handful of berries from the top of the bucket. "Can I take a couple of these?"

"Have as many as you like," Millie said. "But don't you think they would be better with cream?"

"I don't mean a couple of berries. I mean a couple of buckets. I think I could sell them in town."

"You might as well try," Marcia said. Cyril went whistling down the road, a pail in each hand.

"Ten cents a bucket," he said when he returned. "I sold one to an old man on a boat. He didn't have any teeth, but he could eat those berries all right. And Mr. Monocker said I could sell them from his store, too. He thinks everybody will want to put some up for the winter."

"Ten cents!" Millie made him show her the coins. "A barrel of flour is seven dollars. That's . . ."

"Seventy buckets," Cyril said. "I could sell that many, if you could pick them."

Cyril presented the plan at the supper table that night.

"We picked five buckets in one morning," Millie pointed out. "And we could have done ten, if we'd brought that many buckets. We won't have to go far into the marsh, Mamma," she said quickly, seeing the look on Marcia's face. "The berry bushes are just over the stream, the same place we were picking before."

It was agreed that the girls would spend the week picking berries while the boys helped Stuart with the woodpile. The only member of the family unhappy with this arrangement was Bobforshort, who was not allowed to follow them to the marsh any more. He had to be content with watching Cyril as he cut wood. Fortunately, there was a family of chipmunks in the woodpile to keep Bob occupied.

In the afternoons, Cyril loaded Ru's wheelbarrow full of berry buckets and pushed it to town. By the third afternoon, the fun of spending the day outside had worn off, and even Millie was tired of the stained fingers. Nothing in the hot, sticky work kept her mind from wandering to Charles or wondering about Gordon, and she tried to discipline her mind to pray for them, instead of wondering and worrying. Cyril, true to his word, was selling every bucket of berries they picked, going first to the docks along the river and selling to the passengers and crew of the boats, and taking the remains to Mr. Monocker's store.

Marcia had taken over the evening reading of *The Swiss Family Robinson*, and it was just as well, as Stuart was exhausted from the hard labor of felling trees.

"Why did God let the tornado come?" Zillah asked one evening after Marcia laid the book aside. "And if He has enough money to send two thousand dollars to buy the freedom of Luke and Laylie, then why can't He send some money to us? I know many people in town who do not live as they should, and they were spared the tornado. The Monockers—"

"Zillah!" Marcia said quickly. "Remember that our Lord does not like gossip!"

Zillah lowered her eyes. "I know, Mamma. But why can't we have what other people have?"

"You mean why can't you have new dresses," Ru said, not too kindly. "You think of yourself too much. Fan doesn't even have shoes for the winter, and you don't hear her crying."

"I don't like shoes," Fan said seriously. "I want moccasins, like a mountain woman."

"That may change a little, when the snow covers the ground," Stuart said. "But I think I am the richest man in Pleasant Plains."

"But our house . . ."

"If it were our house," Stuart said, "I would be very worried indeed. But it's not." He flipped through the Bible to Psalm 24, and began to read:

> *The earth is the LORD'S, and everything in it,*
> *the world, and all who live in it;*
> *for he founded it upon the seas*
> *and established it upon the waters.*
> *Who may ascend the hill of the LORD?*
> *Who may stand in his holy place?*
> *He who has clean hands and a pure heart,*
> *who does not lift up his soul to an idol*
> *or swear by what is false.*
> *He will receive blessing from the LORD*
> *and vindication from God his Savior.*
> *Such is the generation of those who seek him,*
> *who seek your face, O God of Jacob.*

Annis had drawn close to Stuart's knee as he read. "Is this the hill of the Lord, Pappa?" she breathed. "Is He going to visit us?"

"I hope and pray so every day," Stuart said, lifting her onto his lap.

"Paul quotes the first line of that psalm in 1 Corinthians 10:26," Millie said. "But isn't he speaking of meat sacrificed to idols?"

"Yes," Marcia said. "His meaning was clear—*everything* belongs to God, and we should thank Him for it."

"Do you thank God for everything, Mamma?" Fan asked. "Even Bobforshort?"

To Millie's surprise, her mother pinked. "I am working on that one," she said.

"I still don't understand." Zillah was looking defiantly at Ru. "I don't see why He hasn't blessed us then! I'm sure there is no one in Pleasant Plains like you, Pappa. And Mamma is always feeding the poor and caring for widows and orphans. He said He would give us our daily bread! Oh, this is hopeless! I'm sure you don't understand!" She dropped her knitting as she ran from the room.

Marcia and Stuart both stood up. "I'll go," Marcia said. "I think more may be troubling her heart than berry stains on her fingers."

~

Bob, perhaps sensing in his dog way that it would be their last adventure in berry-picking, was determined to follow Fan into the marsh the next day.

"Come on, boy," Cyril called when the hound started down the path after the girls. "Come on back."

Bob pretended he didn't hear.

"Bob!" Cyril called again.

Fan turned and pointed her finger at the hound. "Go with Cyril," she said. Bob tucked his tail between his legs and crept a little closer to Fan. "You can't come with me," Fan said. "You get all muddy and it makes Mamma mad."

"I'll get a rope," Cyril said. The girls waited until he returned from the barn with a length of light rope and put a loop around Bob's head. Cyril led the dog away. "I'm gonna hafta tie you up." Bob hung his head like a condemned man.

"It's your own fault," Millie told him. "You shouldn't burst through doors."

They had already picked the berries close to home, and Millie led the expedition deeper into the marsh. One more day of berry-picking and they would have enough for the barrel of flour. The early September weather was still hot, and Millie set down her last bucket. It was full. Adah and Zillah had been talking more than picking and still had at least half a bucket to go.

"I'm tired, Millie," Adah said. "Can't we go home now? We can start earlier tomorrow when it's not so hot."

Millie looked at the half-full buckets and sighed. "All right." She put her parasol over her arm and picked up both of her buckets. "Where's Fan?"

"Here I am." Fan's voice drifted over the bushes.

"Get your things together," Millie said, putting down the buckets. "I'll get Fan."

Fan had found the largest patch of berry bushes Millie had ever seen, just around the corner from where they had been picking.

"Fan!" Millie scolded. "You know you are not supposed to wander out of sight!" Just then the breeze shifted, blowing toward Millie across the berry patch, and the hair on her neck prickled. There was something pungent on the breeze, a musky smell Millie had not encountered before.

"Fan, it's time to go."

"But Millie, look!" She held up her overflowing buckets, and as she did, something huge reared up from the berry bushes behind her.

CHAPTER

5

# Here There Be Monsters

*My command is this: Love each
other as I have loved you. Greater
love has no one than this, that
he lay down his life for
his friends.*

JOHN 15:12–13

illie stifled a scream as the bear rose to its full height. It lifted its nose to the air, sniffing the breeze. *If I can smell the bear, surely it will smell Fan! But no, the wind is blowing in the wrong direction.*

"Come here right now, Fan!" Millie commanded.

Fan looked hurt. "But Millie! I —"

"I said right now!" Millie snapped. Fan started toward her, dragging her feet. The bear swung its head from side to side, nose testing the air. Gordon had told her that bears had very poor eyesight. *Or was that porcupines? Oh, God, let this bear have poor eyesight,* Millie prayed. *What else did Gordon say about bears? Don't scream, don't run. A bear can outrun you.* The bear was still on its hind feet, tasting the air with a pink tongue, when Fan reached Millie. Millie took her sister by the shoulders so she couldn't turn around.

"I need you to be very brave and promise me you won't scream," Millie said.

Fan looked disgusted. "I never scream. What are you looking at?" Fan twisted away from her and turned around. She pressed back against Millie at the sight of the bear. "Millie!"

"Shhh. Put your buckets down." Millie tried hard to keep her voice calm, not wanting to panic either Fan or the bear. "I'm going to give you a piggyback ride, but we have to move slowly."

The bear seemed to be looking right at them now. It dropped to all fours and came through the berry bushes, stopping to rake at the dry grass with one huge paw. Millie lifted Fan onto her back and started to edge away. The bear followed. Millie stopped, and the bear opened its mouth to show huge fangs.

"I *might* scream," Fan said.

"No," Millie said firmly. "You *must not*. Close your eyes now so you can't see. Are they closed tight?"

"Yes, Millie."

Millie gripped her parasol and took another step backwards. *Bears won't attack you if they can't figure out what you are* — it was almost as if Gordon was speaking in her ear. *I am a very frightened person with a child on her back,* Millie thought. *And nothing but a parasol in her hands! Lord, show me what to do* . . . the prayer was no more than formed when the bear charged, covering the distance more quickly than Millie could believe.

"Lord, help us!" Millie shouted, snapping her parasol open in its face. The bear swerved, passing so close she felt it brush her hand, and retreated.

"I'm scared, Millie."

"Hush," Millie said, intent on the bear. There was something trying to get into her brain, something . . . a deep sound of baying echoed through the marsh. *Bobforshort!* He was on a trail. *Please, God,* Millie prayed, *let him be trailing Fan! Let him be coming here.* She kept the parasol open, holding it above her head in an attempt to look larger. It seemed to confuse the bear, or at least make it more wary. It pawed the ground, then turned its head as Bob's bugle sounded again, closer than before. *He's coming! He's trailing Fan!* The bear raked at the ground once more.

"Millie, it's going to . . ."

The bushes beside Millie exploded and Bob shot past, his hackles raised and fangs bared. The bear met him with a roar that seemed to shake the very ground.

Millie turned and ran as fast as she could up the hill to where she had left her sisters. They were huddled together, arms around each other, berries spilled around them. They had heard the roar but could not see the bear through the thick bushes.

"Millie!" Adah cried. "What is it? What made that noise?"

"Run!" Millie shouted, dropping Fan from her back and pushing them ahead of her toward the trail. "Run for home!" The sounds of a battle raged behind them, snarls and roars, crashing in the brush, and then silence. *Has the bear gotten away from Bob? Is it following us?* A deep-throated bay, and the battle was joined again.

"There's the bridge," Zillah said. "We're not far."

Just as Millie's feet touched the wood of the bridge, she heard a yelp that turned to a scream.

"Bob!" Fan's scream echoed the dog's.

"Don't stop," Millie said. "Keep running."

"What's wrong?" Stuart asked when they burst through the door. Millie tried to tell him, but running all that way had taken her breath. Marcia came in from the kitchen, flour still on her hands.

"A bear, Pappa!" Fan said, gasping for air. "A big bear. It chased us, and Bob is fighting it!"

"Bob!" Cyril jumped up. "Where?"

Fan started to cry.

Stuart caught Cyril by the suspenders as he started for the door. "You can't go after a bear without a gun, son," he said. "Let's get some men to help. We will find Bob, if he isn't home by that time."

Millie realized that she was sobbing as Marcia pried the parasol from her hand. She hadn't remembered folding it, or carrying it while she ran.

# Millie's Great Adventure

It took almost an hour to round up a hunting party. Wallace Ormsby organized the group of men, each with a heavy musket, and they set off down the trail. The women gathered in the yard as the men set out, Cyril, Don, and Ru walking close to Stuart, Reverend Lord looking grim and determined.

"Don't worry, Marcia," Celestia Ann said, "they're loaded for bear." But her eyes followed the tall figure of her husband.

"Loaded for bear or not, they still have a job on their hands," Mrs. Roe said. "Musket might not stop a bear, unless you hit him just right." The ladies went back inside, talking quietly.

"Celestia Ann, it appears to me that you are about ready to birth that baby," Mrs. Prior said.

"I hope so," Celestia Ann said. "Everything is ready at the house."

Mrs. Roe looked at Celestia Ann critically. "I expect she's got a few weeks yet, although I'll make sure I'm available." Mrs. Roe delivered the babies of Pleasant Plains, and she was also the best animal doctor in town. She could stitch them up or set a leg as needed. When she'd heard that Bob was in a bear fight, she'd come with her husband, bringing a bag full of catgut for stitching, bandages, and medicines from her herb garden. Talk of babies and births continued over tea in the kitchen, but Millie couldn't help but notice that Celestia Ann glanced out the window every few moments. "Here they come!" she said at last.

The gangly form of Matthew Lord was walking in front, but as he turned to hold open the gate, Millie put her hand to her mouth. Cyril walked behind him, something limp and lifeless in his arms. Stuart and the rest of the men were behind him.

"Don't look like I'll need my bag," Mrs. Roe said, shaking her head.

"No!" Fan ran out the front door to meet them, then Cyril walked right past her. He sat down on the step with Bob cradled in his arms.

"Oh, Cyril," Marcia said. "I'm so sorry." Fan was crying silently. Stuart and Ru went to the barn for shovels and then walked to the bottom of the garden.

"Too bad about your hound," Mr. Roe said, as Celestia Ann came to take Matthew's hand. "I figure he saved at least one life today. Bear hit him more than once, but he kept on coming. You could read it in the tracks. That dog had no give-up in him."

"Do you think the bear will come back?" Marcia asked.

"Him?" Mr. Roe scratched his head. "Not for a while. He'll be in the next county tomorrow. A bear'll cover sixty miles in no time at all. There's plenty of space out there for him where there are no people, and that's where bears like to stay. It was just bad luck your girls ran acrost him."

The hunters, with the exception of Wallace and Matthew, said their good-byes, and the whole family gathered around as Bob was buried.

"I'm sorry, Cyril," Fan said at last, burying her head in his stomach. Cyril wrapped his arms around her.

"Don't be a baby." It was the first time he had spoken since they arrived, and his voice was hoarse. "Bob hated it when you cried; it made him howl, you know it did. You think he'd want to see you blubbering over his grave?" He wiped his nose on his sleeve and looked up at the sky, blinking hard.

No one had an appetite for dinner that night, or for reading from *The Swiss Family Robinson*. As the gloaming settled over the hill, Millie stole away to her old swing under the huge tree. She could see the plot of freshly turned dirt from where she sat, and she let the tears run down her face for the dog, for Cyril, for Fan. It could have been Fan. *Everyone dies, Lord, I know. Even the finest houses and education cannot keep death away. It comes for us all. It can come more suddenly on the frontier, that's all.*

Millie had cared for the sick and helped prepare bodies of friends and neighbors for burial, and Mrs. Roe delivered the babies of Pleasant Plains, but it was Marcia Keith who held the hands of the dying, speaking words of courage and faith.

Millie caught a flash of movement from the corner of her eye. Marcia was walking through the roses, stopping now and then to snip a bloom, then placing it in the blue vase she carried. Finally satisfied, she knelt in the grass and placed the vase at the head of the small grave and folded her hands. Millie sat quietly, not wishing to disturb her mother's prayer.

*Here there be monsters.* Millie looked at the words neatly written in her prayer journal. *It's true, Lord. It takes courage to face life, and I know that courage can only come from You. I feel like writing a psalm of praise and a psalm of grief all at once. I want the kind of courage Bob had, to face whatever comes, to lay down my life for my loved ones. Bob laid down his life in one heroic act. How could one hound possibly think he could fight a bear? I wish I could draw him from memory for Fan and Cyril, draw the hound God intended, with droopy ears and a lion's heart.*

Millie stopped to wipe a tear; then she dipped her nib in the inkwell again and began to write. *I confess I didn't feel a bit brave when facing the bear. Could I lay down my life to save another? Mamma lays down her life for us bit by bit, every day, and that takes more courage, I think. I'm sure she never imagined living in a place with bears when she married Pappa. She never dreamed of living on the frontier. It must take great courage for her to face each day.*

"Millie?" Fan was peeking in her door. "Can I sleep in here tonight?"

"Of course," Millie said. "I was just getting ready to go to sleep myself."

Fan ran across the bare floor and jumped into the bed, pulling the covers up over her eyes.

"What are you doing?" Millie asked.

"I don't want to see when you damp the light," Fan said in a small voice. "It makes everything look lumpy."

*Like bears*, Millie thought, looking at the curved back of her chair. She put away her pen and ink, blew out the lamp, and crawled into bed. Fan shivered against her back.

"Bob was a good dog, wasn't he?"

Pictures of muddy tracks and broken vases passed through Millie's mind. "Yes, he was a good dog."

"Do you think dogs go to heaven?"

"I don't know," Millie said slowly. "But I do know that Jesus is very good, and we can trust Him. There are lots of things we will have to ask Him about when we get there."

"I'm going to ask Him about Bob," Fan said. "That's the first thing I'll ask."

Millie couldn't help but smile, imagining Fan standing before Jesus. *What I want to know is . . .* Fan was quiet for a moment, and then, "Cyril wouldn't have let that bear kill Bob. Cyril would have figured out a way to save him."

"There was nothing we could do, Fan. Not one thing."

# CHAPTER

# Guns and Fish

*Taking the five loaves and the two
fish and looking up to heaven, he
gave thanks and broke them....
They all ate and were
satisfied....*

LUKE 9:16–17

# Guns and Fish

*W*allace Ormsby carried his musket up the hill to the Keiths' house three days later. Don and Ru followed him into the parlor, and Cyril arrived a few moments later, as if the gun had some mysterious magnetic force to pull him in from the woods.

"Stuart," Wallace said, "I've been thinking it would be wise for you to borrow my muzzle loader. That bear might be in the next county, but it might not. Here on the edge of the marsh, you never know what you will encounter."

"I had thought of it," Stuart admitted. "The boys need to learn to shoot and I was planning to teach them, but somehow after Gordon's accident, I had no heart for it. They should learn. We are on the frontier." He said the word as if it had just occurred to him, the wildness and the danger of the place to which they had come.

"And me, Pappa," Millie said. Millie had never been fond of firearms, especially not after Gordon's accident. She much preferred to draw wild creatures rather than to hunt them. But Fan had been her silent shadow every day since the attack, and her quiet presence as well as the grave at the foot of the garden were enough to remind her of what might have been. She was quite sure she would shoot a bear before she allowed it to reach Fan.

Stuart set down his cup. "I never considered that my daughters might have to shoot bears."

"Celestia Ann is a very good shot." Millie filled his cup again from the pot on the stove. "Many girls hunt in order to put meat on the table. And Aunt Wealthy can shoot a rifle."

"That's true, Stuart," Marcia said. "Wealthy did go tiger hunting in India with her brother."

Stuart agreed at last. Wallace led the whole tribe of Keiths to the field beyond the barn. Millie took along her sketchpad. She drew an outline of a bear as Fan watched intently. Millie tore out the page and carried it to a fence-post about twenty-five yards across the pasture.

"That will take a good shot," Wallace said, measuring out the gunpowder, pouring it into the barrel of the musket. "Are you sure you would not like the target closer?"

"I'm quite sure I would not like a bear any closer," Millie said, watching the preparation of the musket intently. Wallace put in a small piece of cloth to keep the powder in place, then tapped it down with the ramrod. He wrapped the round lead shot in a cloth patch to hold it in place, then rammed it over the powder. He poured gunpowder into the fire hole and pan, and cocked the hammer.

"When I release the trigger," he explained, "the flint on the hammer causes a spark. This ignites the powder in the pan, and that burns down the fire hole to the charge behind the musket ball." He held the musket to his shoulder, sighted down the barrel, and pulled the trigger. There was a clack and a flash, a slight delay, and then a huge roar. Don and Cyril shouted.

"That's amazing!" Zillah said, but Fan was squinting at the target.

"You missed," she said.

"How can you tell from here?" Zillah asked. Fan shrugged, but as Wallace set about loading the musket again, Ru ran to the target. He leaned over and examined it, then stood and spread his hands.

"No holes," he shouted. He was back by the time the musket was ready to fire again.

# Guns and Fish

Again Wallace held it to his shoulder and sighted down the barrel. It roared, and Millie could see the paper jump.

"Hit the corner that time," Fan said. Don and Cyril ran to the target to examine it. Their shouts confirmed that he had hit the paper but missed the picture on it.

"Not a bad shot," Wallace smiled. "If I do say so myself. You must have a strong arm and a steady hand, to say nothing of a good eye to make a clean shot." He loaded the musket, then offered it to Millie. Fan edged closer to watch. The musket was much heavier than Millie had expected. She held it up, sighting down the long barrel. Suddenly the memory of the bear's charge washed over her, and she let the rifle down, her heart beating wildly. The bear was too huge, too savage. It would be on her too fast. Millie could feel herself shaking.

*Your servant has been keeping his father's sheep. When a lion or a bear came and carried off a sheep from the flock, I went after it, struck it and rescued the sheep from its mouth.* The shaking stopped as Scripture filled her mind. *When it turned on me, I seized it by its hair, struck it and killed it.*

"Millie? Are you unwell?" That was Marcia's voice.

"I . . . I'm fine, Mamma." She lifted the musket once more.

"Hold it snug to your shoulder," Wallace said. "It kicks when it fires. The explosion, you know."

Millie pulled it into her shoulder, careful to keep her finger off the trigger. She sighted at the paper, finding the black blob in the middle of it with the bead on the end of the musket barrel. *I went after it, struck it and rescued the sheep from its mouth.* She let out her breath slowly, then held it as she pulled the trigger. The stock slammed against her shoulder as it roared.

"Millie, you did it!" Fan cried. "You got it!"

77

"Now, Fan," Zillah said, "you can't possibly tell that from this distance."

"Yes, I can!" Fan said. "Millie nailed it."

Cyril and Don ran to confirm this; they pulled the paper off the post and ran back with it. There was a neat round hole through the center of the bear.

"Millie nailed it clean," Cyril said. "That's one dead weasel."

"Bear," Millie corrected. "It's a bear. But perhaps it was beginner's luck." This time she loaded the musket herself, Wallace watching over each step. The paper was returned to the post, and again Millie raised the gun to her shoulder. Blam!

"Got him again," Fan declared. Wallace's face was turning a bit pink.

"I think that is enough for me today," Millie said. "Let the boys take their turns. My ears cannot take much more of this." It was true, her ears were ringing. Fan skipped happily beside her all the way back to the house.

The musket hanging over the kitchen door was the topic of much conversation that night, with Don and Cyril describing the shots they had taken.

"None of us did as well as Millie," Ru admitted.

"If Wallace had known it was a bear," Zillah said, "he would have hit it, too."

"What possible difference could it make whether it was a bear or a weasel?" Stuart asked.

"Pappa!" Zillah said, as if explaining to a child. "A bear is much larger than a weasel, so it's easier to hit."

"I see," Stuart said. "That must explain it then."

*Keeping a steady aim would be a good bit harder if a bear were charging me,* Millie thought. *One shot. That is all I would have, and no time to reload before the bear would be upon me.*

# Guns and Fish

When Fan was not spending time with Millie, she spent her hours with Glory and Esther.

"Isn't there some way we can keep them, Pappa?" Millie asked one night after the children had gone to bed.

Stuart shook his head. "I wish I could find a way. But it's better to sell them after the first hard freeze, as we had planned."

Autumn traced maps on the leaves, red and yellow roads along the veins, then decorations on the edges. It was beautiful and somehow frightening all at once. *The Swiss Family Robinson* seemed to be doing better than the Keiths, but as Adah pointed out, they got to live in a tree, and didn't have to worry about snow and freezing temperatures.

The whole town knew of the straits the Keiths found themselves in, and while no one offered charity, there was suddenly an abundance of things that people wanted to share. Mrs. Prior discovered that her hens were laying far too many eggs, and brought by a basketful. Millie prepared the soda water for the vats and submerged the eggs to preserve them for the winter.

Celestia Ann's mother sent bushel bags of popcorn—more, Millie was sure, than they could ever eat. Marcia began popping it for breakfast to conserve flour. Millie couldn't say it was delicious with milk poured over it, but it did fill the stomach.

Stuart traded legal work to the mill for new lumber, and Mr. Roe helped him build a smokehouse, a little hut with a hole in the roof at the back. In the center of the dirt floor was a pit for a slow, smoky fire. Still more wood was gathered, hickory and savory woods that would add delicious flavor to the fish as the smoke and heat dried them.

# Millie's Great Adventure

Ru helped Millie set up a table for preparing the fish down by the river; Don and Cyril brought six large fish for their first day's work. Celestia Ann showed Millie how to prepare a brine mixture "thick enough to float a fresh hen's egg" for salting the fish. "You will want to do your work down by the dock," Celestia Ann said. "It's not the sort of job you would want done in your kitchen."

Fan made a gagging noise as Millie split the first fish.

"Very good," Celestia Ann said. "Now you just rinse it with fresh well water, and then put it in the brine to soak for a couple of hours."

Fan made a louder noise, just in case Millie hadn't heard the first.

"Why, Fan Keith," Reverend Lord said. "I'm surprised at you!"

Millie had to smile at the way her sister jumped. She hadn't seen Matthew Lord coming down the hill.

"Hello, dear." He took Celestia Ann's hand. "Marcia said I would find you ladies down here." There was a slight emphasis on the word ladies, and Fan frowned.

"Ladies don't have to like fish," she said.

"Of course not," Reverend Lord agreed. "However, I thought *you* liked mountain men."

"Mountain men?" Fan asked.

"Of course." Celestia Ann winked at Millie. "How do you think a mountain man survived through the winter? He ate dried fish and jerky!"

"Is that Gospel?" Fan asked.

"It's not in the Bible," the good reverend said, "but it is true."

Celestia Ann laughed. "My own grandpa was a mountain man. How do you think I learned to do all of these things?"

"Wait here." Fan ran back up the hill.

"*Solomon Tule, Mountain Man,*" Millie explained, flicking a fish heart from her knife. "She keeps that book under her bed, where Don and Cyril can't find it. Solomon Tule is the ultimate expert on all the doings of mountain men."

"And how is Fan faring?" Matthew asked.

"She seems to be better," Millie said, "but her relationship with Cyril . . . he may have forgiven her, but she hasn't forgiven herself, and so she can't believe he has." They talked quietly for half an hour before Fan reappeared.

"Mountain men do smoke fish," she announced. "So I guess I will too."

"Excellent," Millie said, throwing the last pail of fish remains into the river. "In two hours you can help me take out all these fish and put them on racks in the smokehouse."

Fan did help, and even added "keep the slow fire going" to her list of chores.

Cleaning the fish Cyril and Don caught became Millie's daily chore, and one she dreaded, although she would not admit it. Although she washed thoroughly with brown soap when she was done, she suspected that a whiff of fish smell hovered over her wherever she went. As she added new racks of fish to the smokehouse, she took out those that were completely dried. Some she ground into powder to add to soups and stews, and others she wrapped in brown paper and kept in the cool, dark pantry.

The world seemed to teeter between summer and fall, unwilling to leave the one and commit to the other, but finally came the morning when Marcia had to break ice on the water bucket by the back door.

"You will need to take Glory and Esther to the Joneses' this afternoon, Ru," Stuart said. Fan looked up quickly, then back at her bowl of popped corn and fresh milk. "Mr. Jones will be paying in cash," Stuart continued. "I was thinking perhaps Fan would like to go to town to get a new pair of boots? I'm sure it will snow soon."

"No," Fan said, then flushed. "I don't care if my toes freeze off. I just don't care!"

"Fan Keith!" Marcia sounded shocked. "You will apologize to your Pappa this instant!"

"I'm sorry, Pappa," Fan said.

That afternoon Millie sat in her swing with her sketchpad. She had seen Fan's little face peeking from the window when Ru led the horses away. *Why does the frontier have to be so hard on Fan? Lord, I don't understand why You let these things happen. Why does life have to be so hard on all of us? Charles hasn't written me in weeks. Has he forgotten me? Have You forgotten me?* "I don't like popcorn for breakfast," Millie said aloud. "If You would like to know, Lord, I did like the breakfasts at Roselands. Piles of waffles, sweets and tarts, eggs, toast . . ." Her mouth watered even speaking the words.

"Don't cry for onions."

"Ru! I didn't know anyone was listening."

"Just got back," he said, sitting down beside her. "And of course you knew someone was listening. Just like I know it when I'm working on my garden all alone. Jesus is always listening when you speak to Him."

Ru had grown tall, and thoughtful, too, over the year Millie had been gone. He spent a great deal of time working alone, and more reading his books. When Stuart was home, Ru was at his right hand, doing anything that needed to be done.

"What did you mean about onions?"

"When God led the children of Israel out of Egypt, He provided special food."

"Manna," Millie said. "I remember."

"But the rabble among them were not satisfied. They cried for onions and fish and cucumbers, melons, leeks, and garlic—all the things they had eaten when they were slaves in Egypt. He wouldn't have fed them manna forever. It was just a season. This is a season, too, and seasons pass."

"Ru," Millie said, suddenly remembering a conversation they had had when she first returned home, "do you still want to be a doctor?"

"I want to help people," Ru said. "But I'm not sure I want to be a doctor. The more I read Dr. Chetwood's books, the more interested I become in the mixing of medicines. I think I would like to have my own pharmacy. Perhaps even discover new cures. One thing I do know. My hopes and dreams are on the other side of winter. We have to work hard now to make it through."

"How did you grow so wise?" Millie asked.

"If anyone lacks wisdom, let him ask God," Ru quoted. "I ask every day. I read one verse each morning, and I think and pray about it as I work, asking God to help me understand. That's why I like to work alone. I talk to Him all day long. Sometimes . . ." He looked at her with earnest blue eyes. "Sometimes I'm sure God tells me things, Millie. When I'm praying. It's a feeling inside, but more than that. A sureness and a peace." He looked as if he wanted to say more.

"Has God told you something lately?"

"Yes," Ru said, standing up. "It's going to be all right."

"You mean we will make it through the winter?"

"I don't know about that," he shrugged. "I mean with Charles Landreth."

A chill went down Millie's spine.

"It's going to be all right. Well, I have work to do." He turned and walked away.

*My hopes and dreams are on the other side of winter.* Millie felt as if the world had turned around, and Ru was suddenly her older brother. *We are all growing up. How could I have forgotten that spring comes only after winter?* She kicked her feet as she swung until her toes almost touched the treetops.

"Millie Keith!" The shocked faces of Lu and Helen looked up at her.

"What if a young man had been walking with us? It's scandalous, a young woman your age flying through the air like that!" Helen said.

**7**

# Of Suffering
# and Servanthood

*Now faith is being sure of what
we hope for and certain of
what we do not see.*

HEBREWS 11:1

# Of Suffering and Servanthood

*T*he world slowly turned from the glorious reds and golds of September. Millie grew used to eating popcorn for breakfast, smoked fish and corn dodgers for dinner, and smoked fish, greens, and white bread with butter for supper each and every day. It was odd to see the dandelion greens, or wild asparagus, served on Marcia's fine china, although Millie had eaten it often at the Lightcaps'.

Not even Fan complained about the fish anymore, but the delicious fruit that the Swiss Family Robinson ate in their adventure made Millie's mouth water when Marcia read. Soon even the greens would be gone, buried beneath a soft blanket of snow.

Millie answered a knock on the kitchen door one morning just as the Keiths were getting up from breakfast. There stood Celestia Ann, a halo of red curls escaping from her bonnet. "Would you care to walk with me, Millie?" Celestia Ann asked. "I was on my way to Mrs. Simon's with a pot of soup."

"I'll ask Mamma if she can spare me for the morning," Millie said. "Won't you come inside?"

"Oh, no! I have mud on my boots, and I would track it into the kitchen. Besides, it's a glorious day! I don't mind waiting here at all."

"And I will add a loaf of bread to Celestia Ann's soup," Marcia said from inside. "Would you like to go with Celestia Ann and Millie, Fan?"

"No," Fan said quietly, and Marcia gave Stuart a worried look over the little girl's head. Fan had hardly touched her popcorn, and she had eaten less than usual during the last few days. Her eyes had grown far too serious for a nine-year-old, as if the thoughts behind them were too sad for words.

"Fan, you can't mope around today," Cyril said, folding his arms.

"I can't?"

"Nope. I need your help."

"*My* help?"

Cyril nodded. "I got a plan," he said. "And you are the only one who can make it work."

"What kind of plan?" Adah asked suspiciously.

"A secret plan." Cyril looked at Stuart. "But it's legal."

"That's a relief," Stuart said, standing up. "Make sure you finish your chores before you set this plan in action."

"Yes, sir. In fact, it has to do with chores. Fan needs to start milking Belle."

"I do?"

"Twice a day," Cyril said.

"That makes no sense," Adah said. "Milking is Ru's job."

"I'll do it," Fan said. "Even when it's cold outside."

"And you can help me with the woodpile, too."

"May I, Mamma?"

Marcia looked at Cyril for a moment and then nodded her head. "You may help Cyril if you like. However, I don't want you neglecting your own chores."

Millie kissed her parents, wrapped a loaf of bread in paper, and slipped out the back door.

"Matthew has gone down to the Lightcaps'," Celestia Ann said as they shut the gate behind them. "And I didn't want to be cooped up like a broody hen for one more minute. I love the feel of the air in autumn."

"Would you like me to carry the basket?" Millie asked. "It must be heavy."

"You are almost as bad as Matthew," Celestia Ann laughed. "Hard work is good for me. It will make the birth go easy."

"Have you decided on names? Will it be Matthew Davy Crockett Lord?"

"Matthew *Peregrine* Lord, after Matthew's great-great-granduncles. *Peregrine* means pilgrim. His uncle was born on the Mayflower."

"And if it's a girl?"

Celestia Ann laughed. "Firstborn children in Matthew's family are always boys. It's tradition."

They turned down the narrow lane that led to Mrs. Simon's. Mrs. Simon and her husband had homesteaded on the land. Mr. Simon had passed away before there was a proper town, or a churchyard for that matter. His headstone stood neglected under a spreading willow tree, remaining there even though his children were buried in the graveyard by the church. A neat picket fence had held the weeds at bay for years, but it was weathered and gray now, and the garden it protected was a tangle of thistles and vines among the roses.

"If I had time," Celestia Ann sighed, "I could do something with this place. Make it look more cheerful and inviting."

"Even if the garden invited, Mrs. Simon would not." Millie stepped over a vine that ran across the path.

"There's something alive about a garden, even in winter," Celestia Ann said. "It's like a promise."

"This one promises to need a great deal of weeding." Millie knocked on the door and then pushed it open, stepping into the small kitchen. All the blinds in the house were drawn tightly shut. The air inside was musty with the smell of mildew.

"Mrs. Simon?" Celestia Ann called.

"Who is it?" a reedy voice called from the back room.

"Celestia Ann and Millie Keith," Millie called. "We've brought you soup and bread."

"It will probably upset my stomach," the woman said. "Dr. Chetwood says I have a delicate constitution."

"If you would rather not have any —"

"I didn't say that! When you are old and an invalid, you must suffer with what you can get."

*Suffer indeed! Celestia Ann makes very good soup. She would have served it to Jesus Himself if He came to visit. And Mamma scrimped on the flour she used for our family's baking so that she would have enough to send a small loaf to Mrs. Simon every few days.*

"Bring it back here," Mrs. Simon said. "I am too weak to get up today."

Celestia Ann ladled out a bowl for the sick woman while Millie cut a thick slice of bread. They carried the meal into Mrs. Simon's room on a bed tray.

"Shall I open the window for you?" Millie asked. "It's a glorious morning!"

"Oh, no. I can't bear the light. Just plump my pillow and help me sit up."

Millie did as she was instructed while Celestia Ann held the tray.

"Let's pray that this soup makes you better," Celestia Ann said as she placed the tray on a pillow on the old woman's lap.

"I'll leave the praying to the minister and the getting better to the doctor," Mrs. Simon snapped. "They've both been to see me, and I must confess I prefer the doctor. He says that my chances have improved. All your husband said was that he didn't want me to die without hope." She sniffed. "I should think he would be worried more about his own household!" She looked meaningfully at Celestia Ann's thickened waist. "You should not be out in your condition. Locked safely in your room — that's where you should be. Don't you know how dangerous it is for the baby for you to waltz around the countryside? All kinds of things can go wrong at this point. If a rabbit crosses your path, your child will have a harelip. Do you want to have that burden to bear for the rest of your life? Don't shake your head at me, young woman! You may think it is ridiculous, but it happened to my sister Dorothy."

"Thank you for your concern. I will try to avoid rabbits," Celestia Ann said solemnly.

The old woman nodded. "We should be concerned with one another."

"I'm sure Matthew was concerned for your soul, Mrs. Simon."

"Not that again! I am far too weak to worry about that right now. Souls will have to wait until I am stronger."

"That's just his point," Celestia Ann said gently. "You may not grow stronger. We should all be prepared . . ."

"You may be even closer to death than I am!" Mrs. Simon snapped. "This is your first, isn't it? That's always the hardest. My younger sister died delivering her first, and the wretched babe followed her. I've lost, oh, I don't know how many friends to childbirth. How close is the dreaded hour?"

Millie glanced at her friend's face. Celestia Ann might be a shade pale, but her smile was just as sweet as ever.

"Any day now. But did you dread the birth of your own children? Surely holding them in your arms was worth the pain and trouble?"

"I think not. What did I gain? They have all gone and left me alone." She paused to slurp soup from her spoon, and then licked her lips. "I was in terrible dread during each of my confinements. Death comes close, so close, in those hours."

"Every person in Pleasant Plains, in America, in the whole world was born," Millie pointed out. "I expect most mothers live through it. God made us that way."

"God? It has nothing to do with God. I am talking about medical science," Mrs. Simon said. "I have spoken to Dr. Chetwood about it, and he assures me that I am right. 'One out of every eight women will die in childbirth,' he said. One out of eight!"

"That means that seven out of eight live." Millie took the tray. "Would you like us to help you get up now? You could walk around a bit, and perhaps feel better."

"No, I would not. Dr. Chetwood said lying in bed would help me regain my strength."

Millie had heard Dr. Chetwood discussing Mrs. Simon's case only days before, and he had not seemed optimistic that the old woman would ever regain her strength. Mrs. Simon must have seen the dismay on her face.

"You may think me pathetic, lying on this bed, but Dr. Chetwood assures me that many people recover from situations far worse than mine!" The old woman gave Celestia Ann a sly look. "Why waste your prayers on me? Pray for yourself, young lady, and tell your husband to do the same. I need nothing from you." She tipped the soup bowl to scrape out the last drop; then she wiped her mouth on the sleeve of her nightgown. "And if I do, I will call."

"No one lives forever," Millie said, not too kindly. "And should you die tonight, wouldn't you want your soul to be ready to meet the Lord?"

"Hush! Oh, hush!" the woman cried. "Don't speak of dying in the night!" She looked around the room almost wildly. "That's when they come!"

"Who comes?" Millie asked, surprised at the woman's obvious fear.

"The breath stealers. It's the nights I fear the most, those dreadful quiet hours all alone!"

"You needn't be alone," Millie said, suddenly touched with pity. "Jesus will be with you. All you have to do is ask."

"Must you torment me?" Mrs. Simon cried. "Can't you see that I am a sick woman? Dr. Chetwood has advised me not to make any trying decisions until my body is stronger, yet that is just what the Reverend wanted me to do. 'Make a decision for Christ.' It's against my doctor's orders. I don't believe I want to talk to you anymore."

"We'd better be going," Celestia Ann said.

"No!" the pitiful thing cried. "Stay a little longer. No one else will be here today, and the hours just drag by."

Millie and Celestia Ann stayed an hour longer, talking of the weather and the happenings around town. Mrs. Simon seemed so improved by the conversation and the soup that she managed to get out of bed. Millie helped her into a fresh nightgown, while Celestia Ann changed the bedclothes.

"You are really too good to me," Mrs. Simon said as they prepared to leave. "I do hope everything goes well with your confinement, and I promise to think more about what you have said just as soon as I am well."

Millie took a deep breath when she stepped out of the door, as if she could breathe in the sunshine.

"Are you afraid?" Millie asked at last, "of having a baby, I mean?"

"A little," Celestia Ann admitted. "My aunt died in childbirth, and the poor babe with her, struggling to be born. My own mother had nine children and never a trouble, but only four lived to see their first birthday. Now look at me!" She wiped a tear from the corner of her eye. "Matthew would be so upset to hear me talk that way. He prays over our little one every single day! Isn't it strange that God has set women to watch over birth and death? Even when our Lord was dying, it was the women who were close, watching over Him. Oh, Millie! Would you mind stopping with me at the Mercantile?"

Millie didn't mind at all and had wanted to suggest it herself, if only she could think of a good reason. *It will be all right. Does that mean there will be a letter from Charles today?* She was determined not to ask, as she didn't want to see the pitying look on Mrs. Monocker's face if there were no letter. Mrs. Monocker insisted on giving Celestia Ann a pickle from the barrel along with her order of sardines, crackers, and tea.

"I have a letter," the woman began, and Millie's heart skipped a beat, "for Gavriel. You might let her know."

"I'll pay the postage." Celestia Ann held out a dime. "We are on our way to the Lightcaps' now. Matthew is shoveling the stables."

"When will that man learn to be respectable?" Mrs. Monocker said with a sigh. "Reverends do not shovel stalls. What will people think if they see him out there, ankle deep and sweating like a dock man? It can't put godly thoughts

in their minds. What will they think the next time they see
him in the pulpit? They'll think of shovels, that's what."

"Then God will rebuke them," Millie said. "He wouldn't
want them thinking about Matthew Lord at all. I believe he
wants them to think about Jesus."

"Hmmf," Mrs. Monocker said, handing over the letter. "I
think you are too religious sometimes, Millie Keith."

When they reached Lightcap's Livery Stable, the
Reverend Lord's fine tenor voice gave evidence not only of
his presence, but of his state of mind.

> *A mighty fortress is our God, a bulwark never failing;*
> *Our helper He amidst the flood,*
> *Of mortal ills prevailing!*

They could see him now over the wall of the thirteenth
stall, wearing his white shirt and suspenders. Whether the
pile of manure in front of him was a flood or a mortal ill was
not clear, but he was making good use of his faith and his
shovel against it. Jedidiah was matching him shovelful for
shovelful, while Jaz sat on the back of the tall gelding in the
next stall, watching.

"Matthew!" Celestia Ann said. "You're working in your
go-to-meeting clothes!"

"It will save no end of time. I have to go calling on Mrs.
Prescott, and she expects the whole minister — boots to button collar." He waved at his hat and coat, hung neatly on a
tack hook. "But are you sure you should be walking?" He
came over to give his wife a kiss, and Millie had to turn
away to hide her smile. The esteemed Reverend Lord had
rolled his pants up to the knees and his thin, white legs pro-
truded from a pair of Gordon's work boots.

# Millie's Great Adventure

"Of course I'm sure," she said. "We have a letter for Gavriel, and we were just going to take it up to the house."

"A letter?" Jedidiah frowned. "I hope it's good news."

"Perhaps Gordon has found Rayme," Millie said, holding her arms out to Jaz.

"That's not the kind I meant," Jedidiah said. Millie looked at him in surprise. She had never heard him say a word against Rayme before. Perhaps he had grown used to Pleasant Plains and wanted to stay.

They found Gavi looking completely out of place and miserable in an apron and skirts, helping Rhoda Jane in the kitchen.

"Would you like some tea, dears?" Mrs. Lightcap poured pretend tea from a cracked teapot and handed a cup to Millie.

"Thank you," Millie said.

"Well, drink it before it gets cold!" Mrs. Lightcap scolded. Millie sipped at air as Gavi unfolded the letter.

"Gordon's found him," she said, sinking into a chair. "Though they haven't met yet. 'I am advised,'" she read, "'that Rayme Romanik has a job on a riverboat named the *Lucky Lady*. I will be catching up with the L. L. next week. Don't forget to add extra grain to the feed when the weather turns cold.' That's all it says."

"Gordon never could write letters," Rhoda Jane sighed.

"Would you like a refill?" Mrs. Lightcap asked, holding up the empty teapot. "You seem to have finished your tea."

"No, thank you," Millie said. "I'm afraid I must be getting home."

"Do you mind walking alone, Millie?" Matthew Lord asked. "I would like to escort my wife home myself. If she is up to stopping at Mrs. Prescott's?"

96

# Of Suffering and Servanthood

"I'm up to anything at all," Celestia Ann said. They both turned to Millie.

"I would mind walking alone very much," Millie said, and laughed at the look of dismay on Reverend Lord's face. "Fortunately, I will have a good escort and good company. Haven't you assured your flock that Jesus is always with us?" Millie said her good-byes, kissing the slightly smudged face that Jaz turned up to her, and promised to send Fan and Annis to play soon.

The moment she stepped outside, Millie was enfolded in a feeling of God's joy in His creation and His mighty presence. Surely God saw all the pain and hurt of the world, heard each pitiful cry. He saw Bobforshort's small grave, and Fan's tears over Glory, and Gordon's pain. But somehow, beneath it all, creation seemed to be vibrating with joy, as if the first word God spoke on the morning of Creation was still sounding around her, a word that held a secret so huge and wonderful that no sadness could stand against it. *What is this feeling, Lord?*

"Now faith is being sure of what we hope for and certain of what we do not see." *That was Hebrews 11:1, wasn't it? Faith. This* knowing *that God has won the victory over sin and death is faith.*

The hymn Reverend Lord had been singing welled up in her heart and Millie sang the words aloud as she walked.

> *A mighty fortress is our God,*
> *A bulwark never failing;*
> *Our helper He, amid the flood*
> *Of mortal ills prevailing,*
> *For still our ancient foe*
> *Doth seek to work us woe;*

*his craft and power are great,*
*And, armed with cruel hate,*
*On earth is not his equal.*

*Did we in our own strength confide,*
*our striving would be losing,*
*Were not the right Man on our side,*
*The man of God's own choosing.*
*Dost ask who that may be?*
*Christ Jesus, it is He;*
*Lord Sabaoth His name,*
*From age to age the same.*
*And He must win the battle.*

*And though this world, with devils filled,*
*Should threaten to undo us*
*We will not fear, for God hath willed*
*His Truth to triumph through us.*
*The prince of Darkness grim,*
*We tremble not for him;*
*his rage we can endure.*
*For lo! his doom is sure,*
*One little Word shall fell him . . .*

Millie smiled. *And that Word was, and is, and ever more shall be Jesus!* Then, realizing that she was just passing Mrs. Simon's lane, her thoughts turned to Mrs. Simon.

*How horrible it must be, Jesus, to be so alone, locked away in that dark, horrible house. Waiting for death while pretending that she will never die. She knows in the darkness of the night. Why won't she simply come to Jesus? There is no one else who could help her now, no one who could give her hope. Forgive me for being angry with her and for my harsh words. Send someone to speak to her, Lord, someone wise as Mamma and as bold as Pappa. Send someone who can love her, even if she is abominable to them.*

"Millie Keith?" Claudina was peering at her from behind a bush. "I . . . I thought I heard singing."

"And so you did," Millie laughed, reaching for her friend's hand. "I was just having a prayer meeting."

"All by yourself?" Claudina asked, looking around.

"Come, let us bow down in worship," Millie quoted, "let us kneel before the Lord our Maker; for He is our God and we are the people of His pasture, the flock under His care."

"We can't kneel here," Claudina said, sounding not at all sure. "People will think we are odd! Kneeling is all very well for your prayer closet or for church, but it isn't done on a common road where anyone could see."

"Well, *I* think it is odd that we do not worship Him everywhere," Millie said. "I think a man named Saul once prayed on a common road. He asked, 'Who are you, Lord?' God answered his prayer."

"I fear your great learning has driven you mad," Claudina said.

"If this be madness, then come, good friend, and join me."

"That's not the right quote," Claudina said, frowning.

"It's heartfelt nonetheless," Millie said, linking arms with her friend.

**8**

# Beyond Justice to Mercy

*Praise be to the God and Father of our Lord Jesus Christ! In his great mercy he has given us new birth into a living hope through the resurrection of Jesus Christ from the dead, and into an inheritance that can never perish, spoil or fade....*

1 PETER 1:3–4

*T*he Keiths' woodpile had reached the eaves of the barn. Cyril, Don, and Ru spent more time fishing now, and Millie practiced with the musket, although there was no sign that the bear would ever return. Fan faithfully milked Belle each morning and spent time following Cyril around each afternoon. There was a dusting of snow early in October, a harsh promise of the winter to come.

Celestia Ann's smile was not quite as bright, but even the baby's refusal to arrive could not dampen the mood of the young ladies of the Bible study. With the Christmas social just over two months away, there was planning to be done. Discussions of decorations, music, and gowns spilled over from Bible study to Sunday school and even to the Keiths' parlor, overtaking the adventures of the Swiss Family Robinson in order of importance. Adah and Zillah had joined in the preparations for the first time, spending hours with Claudina and Millie, giggling and planning.

"Is a sleigh ride very romantic?" Adah asked Claudina at supper one night. The Keiths' table was full, as Wallace Ormsby had come home with Stuart.

"I think it would be the most romantic thing on earth."

Zillah glanced at Wallace, then flushed, but he didn't seem to notice.

"Pumpkin pie is the most romantic thing on earth," Ru corrected, passing a plate of fish. "I will dance with any lady young or old who brings one."

"Cinderella had a pumpkin!" Annis exclaimed. "Her fairy godmother turned it into a coach!"

"Turnip," Don said. Everyone looked at him. "I thought the fairy turned a turnip into a coach."

"That all depends on which version of the story you read," Marcia said. "I have never been fond of turnips. I much prefer to think she had a pumpkin."

"Who cares if it was a turnip or a pumpkin?" Adah asked. "She had a fairy godmother who could turn rags into ball gowns."

"She had evil stepsisters, too," Don pointed out.

"It is beyond me," Zillah said, with a bit of an air, "how a man could read that story and miss the important parts: the gowns, the coach, the prince, living happily ever after . . ."

"Beats me," Don said, folding his arms, "how a girl could read that story and miss the exciting parts—wicked stepsisters and evil stepmother, and all the trouble they caused. They sure didn't live happily ever after!"

"Well, they didn't deserve to!" Zillah said hotly. "They tried to stand in the way of true love! The fairy godmother was not going to let that happen."

"Mamma and Millie are just as good as any fairy godmother," Fan said loyally.

"Amen," Cyril said. "They can make gowns and pumpkin pies!"

"Speaking of happily ever after," Stuart said, "I received a letter from a solicitor representing Horace Dinsmore today."

Marcia put down her napkin, and Millie caught her breath.

"It contained the papers for two slaves. Or, should I say, former slaves?"

A cheer went up around the table.

"You won't have to arrest Millie after all, Sheriff!" Fan said.

"That's quite a relief," Wallace said, smiling. "She is a better shot than I am. How will we get the papers to them?

Aren't they still in danger until the papers are in their hands?"

"And even after that," Stuart said. "Papers can be destroyed. But Horace is an honorable man, and he assures me his wife's family will stand by the sale. I have dealings with a law firm in New York City, and I will send the papers there. We can write to Millie's friend Miz Opal and tell her to pick up the package. That should be safe for all concerned."

"Pappa," Ru asked, "do you think that slavery will ever end?"

"It must end," Stuart said, "or our country will fall. God has blessed this nation from the beginning, but I don't see how He can continue to bless us if we allow this evil to go on." For the rest of the meal they discussed the arguments that raged in legislatures and were stirred from pulpits about whether or not slavery was wrong and what could be done about it.

"Would you like me to walk you to Mrs. Simon's, dear?" Marcia asked at last. The old woman had grown weaker with the onset of cold weather. Marcia and Mrs. Prior took turns sitting with her, keeping a small fire to warm the room and praying that her strength would return.

As Millie opened her mouth to reply, the door flew open and Beth Roe rushed in.

"Miz Keith! My mamma wants to know can you come right now? The preacher's wife is having her baby, and Mamma's afraid it's not turned right. She said she needs help. She said to get you."

Terrible thoughts seized Millie. *Mrs. Roe attends births, but Mamma sits at death beds. Is Celestia Ann dying?* "Go to Celestia Ann," she said quickly.

"Are you sure, Millie?" Marcia asked.

"I want to help, Mamma. I can't help Mrs. Roe," Millie said. "I wouldn't know what to do, but you would."

"I'll go with you, Millie," Claudina said. "I'm sure my mother will allow it."

Marcia nodded. Adah and Zillah were instructed to wash up and put the children to bed. Ru was to walk Millie and Claudina down the hill.

Millie gathered her shawl and cap, and Ru lit two lanterns to light their way. Millie said good-bye to her parents at the gate. She hurried after Ru, but her eyes went back to the dot of light that was her parents' lantern. She could hear Celestia Ann's words: *Isn't it strange how at death and at birth God has set women to watch?*

*Lord*, Millie prayed, *please protect Celestia Ann and her baby!*

Ru and Claudina waited as Millie knocked gently at Mrs. Simon's door. When there was no answer, she opened it and stepped inside. The house was quiet as she made her way to the bedroom.

Mrs. Prior was sitting beside the sick woman's bed. "Millie!" she said in surprise. "I was expecting your mother." In hushed tones Millie explained about Celestia Ann.

"I can't say I approve of your watching here alone tonight," Mrs. Prior said.

"Claudina is here to help me," Millie said, realizing for the first time that her friend had not followed her into the sickroom. "She's in the kitchen, and Ru is at the front door."

"I'm glad you came early," Mrs. Prior said. "I need to be home myself. Things tend to go at sixes and sevens when I'm away, and it's not fair to my boarders."

"How is she?" Millie asked, looking past her at the bed.

Mrs. Prior shook her head. "Weak and short of breath and afraid to go. I can't imagine anybody putting off preparation until the last moment when they know they are going to die, and after that the judgment! But she won't allow Reverend Lord in the house. She won't let anyone say a word about her soul."

Millie could hear the woman's rasping breath as she stepped near the bed. Mrs. Simon seemed to have shrunk since she had last seen her, and her papery skin was gray.

"Millie Keith is here to sit with you," Mrs. Prior told the sick woman. "She'll watch over you and make you comfortable."

"Oh, if only I could be comfortable," Mrs. Simon moaned. "No one knows my pain! Nobody knows what I must suffer!" Millie's eyes filled with tears of pity, and she started to speak, but Mrs. Simon cried out, "Hush! Don't say a word! Don't talk to me! I can't bear it, I can't bear it. I am too weak!"

"Now you just settle back," Mrs. Prior said. "And try to get some sleep. I'll be around tomorrow, or Mrs. Chetwood, and we'll talk then."

"I don't want to be alone!" Mrs. Simon cried.

"I'll be right here," Millie assured her. "Wouldn't you like a cup of tea?"

"Yes, you are very kind. I know you'd help me if you could, but nobody knows what I have to suffer!"

"I'm just going to see Mrs. Prior out," Millie said. "I will be right back."

She joined Claudina and Mrs. Prior by the front door.

"I'm glad you are here," Mrs. Prior was saying to Claudina as she left. "Death watches are not so terrible if you have company." Millie and Claudina glanced at each other.

# Millie's Great Adventure

"Death watch? Mrs. Simon isn't . . . isn't . . ." Claudina asked.

"Dying? Of course she is." Mrs. Prior's voice was so loud that Millie glanced at the ill woman's door, wondering if she had heard. "But then, we all are. Now what you need to do for the poor thing tonight is keep a kettle boiling on the stove. It will ease her breathing. And give her one teaspoon of laudanum if the pain gets too bad — not too much now or you will do her in."

Millie looked at the sturdy brown bottle and spoon lying on the table.

Ru poked his head in the front door. "You all settled here, Millie?" Ru asked. He was uncomfortable at sickbeds.

"Yes," Millie said, "and thank you for escorting us." He nodded and held the door for Mrs. Prior on the way out.

Millie poured the boiling water into the teapot, letting it steep before she carried it into the sick woman's room. "Here is your tea," she said, trying to sound bright and cheery.

"I've changed my mind," Mrs. Simon said. "I couldn't touch it. I feel cold."

"Here." Claudina pulled up the quilt from the bottom of the bed and tucked it in under the woman's wrinkled chin.

"What were you two whispering about in the other room?"

"Celestia Ann is having her baby tonight," Millie said.

"Death —" there was a pause as she coughed "— is a terrible, cold thing. She must be terribly afraid!"

"We can pray for her," Claudina said. "I'm sure God will take care of her."

"Don't waste your breath," Mrs. Simon sighed. "You can use it for better things."

"Are you afraid?" Millie asked gently. "Afraid of death?"

"I'm not dying!" the woman almost shrieked. Then a look of cunning came over her face. "If death comes for anyone tonight, let him come for the baby. Celestia Ann's baby hasn't tasted life. It doesn't know that life is good. Yes, take the baby, not me. I want to live!" She seemed to be speaking to someone in the corner of the room. Chills crept up and down Millie's spine. She could see nothing but shadows in the corner. Claudina was standing with her hand over her mouth.

"Yes, let the baby die!" Mrs. Simon said with venom.

Millie knew that she should not lose her temper with an ill person, certainly not one who was dying, but this was wrong. It was evil. *How could she even think such a wicked thing?*

"Mrs. Simon, stop that at once. You should not say such things!"

"Of course," Mrs. Simon said. "I only talk to Dr. Chetwood about things of such importance. Not snips like you. And the good doctor says that if I take my medicine, I will be fine. 'Take your medicine,' that's what he said. 'And rest, and we will see what happens tomorrow.' How could we see what happens tomorrow if I were dying? I want my medicine."

Millie carefully measured a teaspoon of laudanum, and Claudina lifted the woman's shoulders so that she could sit up to take the medicine and a sip of tea to wash away the bitter taste. After a few moments the woman's face began to relax.

Millie started to leave the room, but Mrs. Simon cried out, "Oh! Where are you going? Don't leave me, I am in awful distress! Rub that liniment on me, won't you?" Millie took the ointment from the dressing table and looked imploringly at Claudina. *I can't,* Claudina mouthed silently.

*Jesus, help me,* Millie prayed silently. *Help me do what You would do.* She took the top from the jar. "Where do you want it rubbed?" she asked.

"On my back," the woman said, groaning as she turned onto her side. "It eases the pain. Oh, why is it so horrible? What have I ever done to deserve this?" Millie pulled up the woman's nightgown and began rubbing the ointment into the wrinkled loose flesh. *Jesus,* she prayed desperately, *I know You love this old woman. Help me to love her.* Mrs. Simon relaxed as Millie worked in the ointment. Soon she was snoring softly. Millie stopped rubbing and pulled the nightgown down and the covers up.

She and Claudina tiptoed out of the room, leaving the door open so they could hear if their patient woke.

"She's horrible," Claudina whispered when they reached the sitting room. "How could she say such a thing about Celestia Ann's baby?" Her eyes were wide. "You don't think it could work like a curse? That the poor little baby will —"

"Of course not," Millie said quickly, before Claudina could finish the thought. "God hears our prayers for Celestia Ann and her little baby. Why would He allow the evil wish of one woman to wash all of those prayers away?"

"Are you sure, Millie?"

"I'm sure." Millie tried to make her voice firm. She was sure of the goodness of God and His love and care for His children. But she felt as if she were in a pool of darkness, as if it filled the house, the darkest point being Mrs. Simon herself.

Millie had watched over deathbeds before, but always with her mother. She had cared for the dying and prepared bodies that were already dead. But she had never felt such anger,

fear, and loathing as seemed to surround Mrs. Simon's house. It filled the corners and seeped through the walls.

"Millie," Claudina said in a small voice, "I am so tired. I just want to lie down on the lounge and cover up. I know I can't keep my eyes open. If you will wake me in two hours, I'm sure I will be better able to help."

"Of course," Millie said. "I will take the first watch." It was easy enough to say, but Millie found that it took all her courage to return to Mrs. Simon's chamber, even while carrying a dim lamp and her Bible. She settled herself in a chair just inside the sickroom door and used the light of the lamp to read her Bible, looking up every few moments as Mrs. Simon tossed, turned, and moaned in her sleep.

She had never felt wider awake. It was strangely solemn to sit there alone, waiting the coming of the angel of death to one who shuddered and shrank at his approach. She spent her time reading and praying, her pleas to the Great Physician going from the safe delivery of Celestia Ann's baby to the healing of Mrs. Simon's sin-sick soul. As time passed, the darkness around her seemed to grow thicker, to press in on her. Why did Claudina have to sleep! How horrible it was, waiting for the last breath.

*You are not alone.* Millie jumped. She had felt that still small voice inside once before, when she had stood in a room where Gordon Lightcap faced death. It had given her a Scripture to speak to Gordon, and that Scripture had led to his salvation.

Millie sank to her knees. "Is that You, Lord?" she whispered. Peace spread through her like warm liquid honey, and the darkness seemed to pull back, away from Millie, away from the lonely bed in the middle of the room. A peace she had felt before.

*Did we in our own strength confide,*
*our striving would be losing,*
*Were not the right Man on our side,*
*The man of God's own choosing.*
*Dost ask who that may be?*
*Christ Jesus, it is He;*
*Lord Sabaoth His name,*
*From age to age the same.*
*And He must win the battle.*

*Jesus,* Millie prayed, *come to this death room! Oh, Lord, win this battle!*

Mrs. Simon woke with a gasp and sat straight up. "What has happened?" she demanded. "Something is different. Has the baby died? Will I live?"

"Yes, Mrs. Simon," Millie said, rising from her knees, "the baby died." She walked over to the bed and sat down.

"Then I will live!" The cunning look was back in the woman's face. "Dr. Chetwood was right!" Millie searched the gray sunken features and the hollow eyes, and somehow, somehow, she could see the child that Mrs. Simon had been long ago. A frightened, angry child.

"Mrs. Simon, you are dying. Anyone who tells you that you are not is lying."

Mrs. Simon's eyes bored into her. "Why should I believe you?"

"Because," Millie said, taking the clawlike hand, "I love you."

"You don't love me," the woman said. "I know who I am. I am a horrible old woman, no good to herself or the world. You cannot love me."

"Look at me," Millie said. "I am telling you the truth. I do love you, and I am not the only one. I know you are selfish and demanding. I know you have lived your life caring only for yourself. And I couldn't possibly love you without God's help." Mrs. Simon's hand began to shake in hers. "I know who you are, and I still love you, because God put His love in me for you. His heart is breaking for you. He loves you so much He would do anything to keep you from death."

"Anything?"

Millie nodded. "The baby did die," she said, "but it wasn't Celestia Ann's baby. Did you go to church at Christmas when you were a little girl?"

"Yes," Mrs. Simon whispered.

"Do you remember a baby there?"

"The sweet little baby in the hay." Mrs. Simon breathed the words.

"That is the baby who died," Millie said.

"That's not true," Mrs. Simon said. "Not that sweet little baby."

"Yes," Millie said. "The sweetest, most innocent baby ever born. And He grew up to be Jesus, and He was innocent still when they hung Him on the cross. He died so you could live."

"There is not one reason why he would have done it. I wouldn't do it! Not for anyone. Certainly not for an old woman who is selfish and cruel."

Millie couldn't think of anything else to say, so she just held the woman's hand and prayed.

"Even if I wanted to come to God," Mrs. Simon said at last, "it's too late. I have nothing to offer Him. Not one thing. So why would He want me?"

"That's just the point," Millie said. "He wants you. Do you remember when you were courting Mr. Simon?"

"Of course I do! No one ever forgets those days!" A great sigh shook her body.

"Why did you want to spend time with him?"

"Because I loved him," Mrs. Simon said, then added after a pause, "because he was wonderful."

"That's why God wants you. He wants to spend time with you because He loves you. The Bible says that Jesus died to bring you to His Father, because you are His treasure."

"I'm not." Tears were running down Mrs. Simon's cheeks now. "I'm full of sin and I know it."

"He died to take that sin away," Millie assured her, putting her arm around her shoulders. "Jesus died to make you beautiful and spotless, without wrinkle or blemish, and part of His own Bride, the Church."

To her surprise, Mrs. Simon began to laugh. "Without wrinkle? Have you seen this face?"

"You will not wear that face forever."

"Because I am dying."

"Yes, you are."

"I know you're telling the truth," the woman whispered. "If I could only believe what you say about Jesus . . . about the Father . . ."

"And there is One more," Millie said, "who could help us now. May I pray for you?" Mrs. Simon nodded. "Heavenly Father," Millie prayed, "I ask that You send Your Counselor, the Holy Spirit, to Mrs. Simon right now. Let Him testify to the truth of Your Son, Jesus, and all that He did, and all that it means for her life."

Mrs. Simon was sobbing quietly now, so Millie just waited quietly.

"I want it to be true," the old woman said at last. "How can I come to Him? I have nothing to offer Him. I am an old bundle of rags and bones! Rags and bones." She sobbed

quietly for a time, and then said, "Please, please let it be true. How do I ask Him? How do I ask Him to save me?"

Millie turned to Romans 10:9. " 'If you confess with your mouth, "Jesus is Lord," and believe in your heart that God raised him from the dead, you will be saved.' "

"How can that be possible?"

"Anything is possible with God." Millie set down her Bible. "When the Bible says 'Believe in your heart,' it means more than believing that Jesus is God. Satan believes that," Millie explained. "It means submitting your heart to Him. Making Him your King."

Mrs. Simon bowed her head. "I am so afraid, God," she prayed. "I want it to be true. I am trying to believe. Please help me to believe!" A shudder went through her. "I am a sinner, I know that. I've sinned against You all of my life, broken Your commandments and broken Your heart. Now if You want me, if You'll take me, I want to come to You. Oh, Jesus, I'm so sorry for what I have done. I do want You for my King!"

Mrs. Simon opened her eyes in wonder. "Millie, it's true! I know it is. He died to save me, and He wants me. Me!" There was so much life in her at that moment, Millie was certain she would live through the night, and for ten years more, besides. "Will you brush my hair?"

"Of course," Millie said, not quite certain what was happening.

"And I want my red dress and my hat!"

Millie helped Mrs. Simon into her dress and brushed her thin white hair and pulled it up in a twist, pinning the hat on top.

"That's better," Mrs. Simon said. "Imagine, going off to meet Him and knowing so little about Him, only that He's wonderful. Will you read to me, Millie?" She settled herself on the bed, the flounces of her red dress around her.

"Do you want your medicine?" Millie asked.

"No, no," Mrs. Simon said. "I want to know as much as I can. Start with Christmas."

Millie started with the Gospel of Luke. Mrs. Simon's eyes grew heavy. Her breathing was steady and even, and Millie kept reading because there was a smile on her face as she slept. As dawn crept closer, Millie noticed that her breathing changed, grew ragged, and then her chest ceased to rise and fall. Still Millie kept reading, straight through the Gospel, through the Crucifixion, right to the Resurrection. The sun was peeking over the horizon when Millie opened the curtains.

"Happy Easter morning, Mrs. Simon," said Millie.

CHAPTER

9

# Times and Seasons

*There is a time for everything, and a season for every activity under heaven: a time to be born and a time to die....*

ECCLESIASTES 3:1–2

*M*illie was coaxing the coals in the woodstove back to life when Mrs. Prior came in the door.

"Well! I didn't have to rush at all," Mrs. Prior said, glancing at Claudina, still sleeping on the couch. "Mrs. Simon is usually very difficult in the mornings." She paused with her coat half off and looked at Millie keenly. "She's passed then?"

Millie nodded. "Has Celestia Ann's baby come?"

"Don't know. I came straight here to help you girls." Millie followed her into the bedroom, now bright with morning sun.

"Why . . . she's smiling!" Mrs. Prior said, leaning over the still form.

"She had something to smile about, just at the last," Millie said. "She met Jesus."

"Praise God!" Mrs. Prior touched the cold hand gently, then brushed away her tear in a no-nonsense way. "Though I'm going to have a few things to say to her one of these days. Imagine waiting to the last minute like that, causing the rest of us no end of trouble!"

"Would you like me to stay and help prepare the body?"

"No, child," Mrs. Prior said. "You spent the night in preparing her soul. Go home and go to bed. I'll find someone to help here, and Mrs. Simon won't mind the hour I'm away to do it."

Millie was relieved. She was suddenly so tired she could hardly walk. She longed for her own bed with sheets that smelled of Mamma's lavender soap.

"Claudina," she said, shaking her friend's shoulder gently. "Wake up."

# Millie's Great Adventure

"Is it my turn to watch?" Claudina asked sleepily.

"No," Millie said with a smile, "it's time to go home." She explained about her sleepless night and Mrs. Simon's death.

"Oh, Millie! I failed you. I left you all alone."

"Pish-tosh," Millie said, picking up her cloak. "I'm never alone, and neither are you." Millie and Claudina said good-bye at the door, going their separate ways. Millie hugged the coat around her and shivered in the cold October morning. She wasn't sure her feet would carry her all the way up Keith Hill until she saw Marcia ahead of her on the path. She picked up her skirts and ran to meet her mother.

"Mamma, is Celestia Ann . . ." She couldn't finish the sentence, but searched Marcia's tired face.

"Celestia Ann is fine, and the baby as well," Marcia said, taking her hand. "Though our good Reverend is in a state of shock. He keeps calling his little girl Matthew." Millie laughed. "We will have to watch over Celestia Ann for a few days." Marcia's voice grew serious. "The baby was breech, and I have known many women to die that way, and the baby as well. But Mrs. Roe would have none of it. I'm sure Napoleon in all his glory never entered a battle-field with such command. She was giving orders to Celestia Ann, to the baby, to me, and reminding God of every promise He had ever made. It was very close, Millie." Millie could feel her shiver. "Too close. Between us, and with the help of God, we turned that baby. Mrs. Roe was in her element, doing what God intended her to do."

"Do you mean He called her to be a midwife?" Millie asked curiously. "Just as He called Matthew Lord to preach?"

"I think He not only made her to do it, but gave her the strength and courage and faith to call on Him and expect an

120

answer when others would have given up. But what am I thinking? How is Mrs. Simon?"

"Two babies were born last night," Millie said. "One into God's Kingdom here, and another into His heavenly Kingdom."

Marcia stopped and studied her daughter's face. "Mrs. Simon accepted Jesus?"

Millie nodded. "And she's gone to be with Him."

Tears welled in Marcia eyes. "This whole morning is like a doxology, one song of praise to God," she said. "How did it come about?"

Millie described her fear and struggles in the night, and the peace and guiding of God that had come over her at last.

"I think God sent you last night for a purpose," Marcia said. "Many people would face down death for a sweet little baby. It takes a special kind of love to face it down for a Mrs. Simon. Jesus' love."

"She was wonderful, Mamma," Millie said, "just at the last. She was the Mrs. Simon God intended. I wish she had lived her whole life that way, and I can't wait to meet her again in heaven."

They each had to tell their stories once more to Stuart and the whole Keith clan before they could collapse into bed. Millie was asleep before she could even appreciate the clean lavender-scented sheets.

<hr>

"What I want to know," Fan said, "is why do they call it a grunting party?"

Millie glanced at Zillah, who blushed, but Marcia took the question in stride. Fan had seen a litter of kittens born at the Prescotts' a few weeks before and rushed home full of questions about how babies came to visit. Marcia had taken her on a walk away from the ears of her brothers, and Fan had come back nodding wisely.

"I suspected Celestia Ann wasn't just getting fat," she told Millie. "I suspected!"

"Having a baby is very hard work," Marcia continued. "Haven't you ever heard your Pappa grunt when he lifts a heavy load? And after you have done a very hard job, don't you like to have a party?"

"Yes," Fan said, "like the party we had when everybody helped build the stable."

"When a lady does a good job having a baby, then we have a grunting party, because the hard work is over."

"Effie's cat didn't grunt. It growled at me, and it breathed like this." She opened her mouth and panted.

"Perhaps it's more difficult having a human baby," Marcia suggested.

Fan considered this for a moment. "I think I'd rather have kittens," she said.

"We'll talk about that in a few more years," Marcia said with a smile.

They were the first to arrive for Celestia Ann's party. The new mother was sitting up in her rocking chair with a quilt tucked around her and her baby on her lap. Reverend Lord hovered over them.

"She is so adorable!" Adah cooed at the baby.

"You are just perfect," Zillah said, as the baby curled tiny fingers around her own.

"Ten fingers, ten toes," Celestia Ann laughed. "Two eye-winkers, one nose! Looks like a keeper," she said proudly.

Marcia peeked over her daughter's shoulder. "Hello again, little one," she said to the baby. And then, to Matthew Lord,

"Since you are going to keep her, has a new name been chosen, or will you continue to call your daughter Matthew?"

"Joy," the Reverend and his wife said with one voice, then glanced at each other. "Joy Everlasting Lord." Celestia Ann offered the baby to Millie.

"Sorrow may last for the night, but Joy comes in the morning!" Matthew Lord quoted.

If it hadn't been for the sweet little face peeking out, and the heat from the tiny body, she would have thought the blanket was empty. Little Joy's face was almost as red as the tuft of hair on top of her head. Her eyes were murky blue the way Fan's had been when she was born—Joy's would no doubt turn bright blue like her father's. She smelled of the sweet oils that Celestia Ann had rubbed into her skin.

"I wish you could have been here, Millie," Celestia Ann said. "It was such a wonderful thing to hear her first cry."

"I'm only too happy to meet her now." Millie tucked the blanket more securely around her.

"And I understand you were about the Father's business two nights ago, Millie," Reverend Lord said. "I will be speaking a few words over Mrs. Simon's grave this afternoon. I must excuse myself to prepare." He gave his baby daughter a kiss before he left.

The ladies of Pleasant Plains started to arrive, arms full of gifts for the new family—quilts and baby clothes, pies and hams. Many came dressed in black, for they would have no time to return home and change before the funeral, but the twinkles in their eyes and smiles on their lips belied the funeral garb.

Celestia Ann was the center of attention. Millie couldn't help but think that the ladies of Pleasant Plains looked like good fairies, each waiting her turn to bestow a gift. In addition to pies and quilts and baby booties, everyone seemed to have a word of advice. Celestia Ann listened patiently to Mrs. Prescott's endless list of things she must never feed the baby. Mrs. Lightcap stepped forward and explained that you could tell if an infant was ill by tapping its stomach; if it sounded like a drum, then you must act quickly, taking a little ear wax and rubbing it on the baby's navel.

"Don't pay any attention to her," Mrs. Prior, the next fairy in line, whispered loudly. "She is not quite right, you know." Celestia Ann nodded sagely, turning her head ever so slightly to wink at Millie. Fan, Emmaretta, and the little girls soon grew tired of the grown-up talk and were sent to play in the yard.

At that moment the door opened and the real star of the afternoon arrived. Mrs. Roe made a grand entrance. Her hair was a bit disheveled, and there were circles under her eyes. If Millie hadn't known better she would have suspected the use of coal smudges beneath her eyes, and certainly she had had ample time to brush her hair since the baby's birth. A chair was hastily drawn up for her, and she collapsed into it.

"It was a very rough night," she said. "I don't know that I have seen rougher."

"How's about the time the Monockers' cow had twins?" someone asked.

Millie was slightly outraged at her friend's being compared to a cow, but it didn't seem to bother Celestia Ann a bit. "Nope," Celestia Ann said proudly. "I was there both times, and this one was rougher!" The ladies laughed.

Mrs. Roe launched into a detailed description of the hazardous labor and turning the baby so she could be born.

More than once, Millie felt herself blushing, but she soon found herself listening as intently as she ever had in Mr. Martin's classroom. *God set women to watch over birth and death.* Surely delivering babies was just as much part of God's plan as seeing poor Mrs. Simon on her way. It was part of life on the frontier.

"It was the mercy of God and the good help of Marcia Keith that they both survived," Mrs. Roe declared at last. "He gets the glory!"

A meal was served, and Millie felt a little guilty passing by the fish pie Marcia had brought and filling her plate with ham, sausage, and potato dumplings.

Finally Mrs. Prior stood up. "It's time to go say good-bye to a friend," she said. Dishes were quickly cleared, Adah and Zillah offered to stay with Celestia Ann and to clean up, and the rest of the ladies went to the churchyard to say good-bye to Mrs. Simon.

The simple pine coffin was already at the cemetery and sat on the back of a wagon borrowed from the Lightcaps. Stuart and Ru had just finished digging the grave, and the boys stood silently with them. Dr. Chetwood was present, as was the sheriff, hats respectfully in their hands. The ladies of Pleasant Plains took their places, as solemn and tearful now as they had been joyful an hour before.

Reverend Lord opened his big black Bible. The ribbon marker swayed in the wind as he looked at the print. He opened his mouth to read but shut it again and shook his head.

"Death is a terrible thing," Reverend Lord said. "It separates us from the ones we love best." Mrs. Roe started crying. The grave of her son Joe was not far away. "I am convinced that it is not natural at all. We were never meant to be separated from those we love." Dr. Chetwood frowned, but Reverend Lord held up his Bible. "I can read right here that death has not always been the state of man. I have had reason to consider this lately, to meditate on it, and to feel its cold touch come close." He paused as if praying, then continued. "As all of you know," he said, "two nights ago, little Joy Everlasting finally made her appearance at my house. I cannot describe to you the feeling of seeing her for the first time, of holding her after waiting so long." He bowed his head for a moment before continuing. "I can only imagine how much greater the Father's love is than my poor human love. With what joy He greeted Mrs. Simon. How He longed for her, looked for her every day, until she decided to be His. I don't know that He sent angels to bring her a robe and a ring or prepare a feast for her. But I do know that two nights ago the angels rejoiced, and His joy was as great as the father of the prodigal. Mrs. Simon is home at last with her loving Father. But like the prodigal, she squandered her inheritance." One of the ladies gasped. "None of us knows how many days we have on this earth. But I know this: I don't want to spend one day of my time slopping pigs in a foreign country. I want to spend each and every hour in my Father's house. And when it comes time to die, I won't change houses at all—I'll simply change rooms, to one with a better view. What about you?" He looked across the small gathering. "Whose house are you in today? How will you spend the days of your life?"

Millie looked around her at the grave markers, young and old: from Mrs. Simon's, not yet set in place, inscribed 1745–1837, to sweet little Amanda Rose's, with less than a year of life carved into cold stone. Less than a year, but God had uséd her to break a cold heart and bring Damaris Drybread into the Kingdom.

"Let us pray," Reverend Lord said. He led them in prayers not for the soul of Mrs. Simon, but for each of their lives, and the lives of their loved ones. Finally the coffin was lowered into the ground and the dirt shoveled over it.

"I don't know what to think about that young man sometimes," Mrs. Prescott said as she gathered her parasol. "Old Dr. Dobbs would never have said anything like that at a funeral. He would have read the service right out of the book!"

"Now, now," Mrs. Chetwood said comfortingly. "Nothing lasts forever. Dr. Dobbs had to retire, you know."

"Thank God," Mrs. Prior said.

"Pardon?"

"I said thank God for Reverend Lord," Mrs. Prior said firmly. "I do every single day."

Millie lingered in the stillness of the graveyard long after the work of filling the new grave was done, thinking about what Reverend Lord had said. *How do I want to spend my days?* She smiled, thinking of Mrs. Roe's excitement while describing Joy's birth.

*Do you mean He called her to be a midwife? I think He not only made her to do it, but gave her the strength and courage and faith to call on Him and expect an answer when others would have given up.*

*What has He made me to do?* Of course Mrs. Roe did not spend all of her time delivering babies. She was a wife and a mother, too, and active in the church. Just as Matthew Lord did not spend all his time in the pulpit. He shoveled stables and prayed over graves as well. Mamma didn't spend all her time serving the poor and the sick. But when she did . . . that was when she glowed. Aunt Wealthy . . . she had done almost everything. But what she liked best was leading people into understanding who Jesus was. A tingle spread over Millie. Gordon Lightcap. Damaris. Rhoda Jane. Laylie. Mrs. Simon. God had used her to speak to all of them about Jesus.

*And I loved it. Even when it was hard and seemed hopeless. God gave me the courage and the faith to speak to all of them. And they accepted the Lord! That's what I am meant for.* Millie felt like shouting. *I am meant to bring people into Your Kingdom, just like Aunt Wealthy does. Aunt Wealthy never worried about the great crowds, just the person sitting next to her.* God gave Aunt Wealthy an incredible love for everyone she met.

*It's going to be all right with Charles.* Millie knew suddenly that it would, even if she never saw him again. It would be all right with Charles, and with Millie Keith, too. Because God had made her a promise. *I know the plans I have for you.*

She looked for a stick, and scratched a hole in the dirt, a tiny grave.

"I know you sent me to Roselands for a purpose, and talking to Charles was part of that purpose," she said aloud. "But I have been praying that *my* will be done—not just that Charles come to You, but that he come to me, too." She took a stub of charcoal from her pocket and wrote on a rock, "M. K.'s Will," then set up the little headstone. "Rest in peace," she said solemnly, filling in the hole.

"I am not going to wait for Charles Landreth." She said it firmly. She realized that she did have the hope, courage, and faith that he would come to God. She would never stop praying for him, confident of the hope that she would see him again in heaven.

Until then . . . she looked over the gravestones, to the horizon. *Here there be monsters . . . and adventures. How could I ever have thought of giving them up?*

CHAPTER

10

# Plots and Surprises

*The plans of the diligent lead to profit as surely as haste leads to poverty.*

PROVERBS 21:5

# Plots and Surprises

utumn seemed to pause and consider before plunging into winter. Old men sat on porch rockers or gathered on boardwalks, basking in Indian summer warmth and predicting snowdrifts and blizzards.

"The caterpillars had more fuzz," they said, or "Watch the squirrels! That's a sure sign." Millie had watched the caterpillars climb up dry stalks and stems and tuck themselves into bedrolls for the winter, and they'd seemed no more or less fuzzy to her. The squirrels, too, acted just as they always did—hurrying to bury acorns and nuts and promptly forgetting where they had put them.

The people of Pleasant Plains were both as comfortable as caterpillars and as busy as squirrels, following the ebb and flow of the seasons just as the wild creatures did. As nights grew longer and days grew shorter, men spent less time hunting or working in the fields and more time home in front of the fire; the women hurried to fill any empty corner left in their pantry with treasures to be brought out on cold winter nights.

Eventually even stage travel slowed as people settled in for the winter, and Gavi was able to take afternoon walks with Millie once more.

"What are you thinking?" Millie asked her friend one day. Gavi stood on the wooden bridge. Millie perched on the rail beside her, watching the water slide away toward the river. Gavi was so still she hardly seemed to breathe.

"I was trying to remember the color of Rayme's eyes," she said at last. "I think they are brown like Gordon's." She dropped a stick over the edge, and the water hurried it under the bridge and out of sight. "Do you ever have trouble remembering what Charles looks like?"

"His eyes are blue." Millie shrugged. "But I am not waiting for Charles Landreth anymore. I am not married to him, after all, and aside from praying for God's best will in his life, I must get on with my own."

"You have completely given him up, then?"

"Completely. I have decided that I am meant to live a life of adventure, following in the footsteps of my Aunt Wealthy Stanhope. I'm sure that I wouldn't be happy any other way—certainly not managing a house and keeping slaves in the South."

"I envy you then." Gavi dropped another piece of stick in the water. This one caught an eddy and twirled in dizzying circles. "How wonderful to make your own decision, to have your own adventures." The stick broke free of the tiny whirlpool and started down the stream. "That's the worst part, Millie. I'm just enough married that I cannot make any plans or think of any other young man, but I'm not enough married to make a life with Rayme."

"I don't see how that can be. Married is married."

It was Gavi's turn to shrug. "Granmarie said it was very like Joseph and Mary. They were engaged under Jewish laws, which is more serious than a *gadjo* engagement of today. If Mary had been found to be unfaithful to Joseph before they came together, she could have been stoned as an adulteress—yet they had not yet lived together as man and wife. It's the same with me and Rayme."

"Do you dream about him?"

"I . . . I dream about Gordon finding him. And of learning why he never came for me. Is there something wrong with me?"

Millie looked at her friend in surprise. "Wrong with you? Don't you remember long ago when Mrs. Hartley told Jaz that she was a princess?"

"Yes, but if . . ."

Millie put her finger to Gavi's lips. "Shhhhh. There are no 'ifs, ands, or buts' in the Kingdom of God. You are His daughter, and that makes you a princess. I only pray that Rayme is worthy of you. He can't love you as much as Jesus does, of course, but if he does not see your true worth, I shall be very disappointed in him."

"But I'm so old!" Gavi said.

"You're only twenty!"

"*Sixteen* is an old maid if you are Romani. The other girls will have been married long ago. Perhaps that is why he never came. Perhaps he would be too embarrassed to stand beside someone my age and finish the ceremony. It's a disgrace."

"If that's what he's thinking, then I trust that Gordon will knock some sense into his head," Millie laughed. "And if he does not, you can join me in spinsterhood. We will travel the world together, lending a hand to those who have need."

"You make spinsterhood sound like the life of Robin Hood."

Millie laughed, remembering Laylie, her green Robin Hood cloak, and her band of Merry Rascals.

"Not at all. I wasn't planning on robbing anyone. I have a very good example of spinsterhood in my Aunt Wealthy. I wish you could have met her, Gavi. Wealthy Stanhope never married, but she has a very full life. She chooses her own way, charts her own course—after praying about it, of course. She has the most incredible faith."

"Doesn't she get lonely?"

"She has friends all over the world, and a best Friend only a prayer away."

"Perhaps I should reconcile myself to that kind of life," Gavi said. "At my age, it might be best."

"Come on, Methuselah." Millie jumped down from the rail. "I promised Jaz and Annis a walk after they were done playing house."

"I am sorry if I seem morose," Gavi said. "This waiting . . ."

"If Rayme was on the *Lucky Lady*, Gordon has found him by now," Millie said, taking her hand. "Surely you haven't much longer to wait."

The finding of Rayme Romanik became more and more important to the young ladies of Pleasant Plains as the days passed with no word. Gordon Lightcap was one of the best dancers in the county, and it was of great concern that he return before the Winter Social. Sincere prayers were offered up, both at the Keith household and at the young ladies' Bible study. There had been no more letters from Gordon, but as Rhoda Jane pointed out, he was not a letter writer.

"I don't know which is more terrible," Gavi sighed. "Waiting or facing the truth."

"I would choose the truth," Millie said. "You will know the truth and the truth will set you free!"

"Of course you would," Gavi laughed. "You are the girl who crawls out of windows to stop runaway stages, fights bears with parasols, and plans to be a spinster for the rest of her life!"

"And who crawled out the other window?" Millie reminded her.

"That was different," Gavi said. "I had to save Jed and Jaz."

It was strange how that terrifying episode had become nothing but images in Millie's mind, and even those were as fuzzy as if it had happened to someone else. She almost wished the account that Jed had written of the incident had not been lost. If she could see the words which had been written just after it happened, would the dry ink make it real again?

"Aunt Wealthy always says that courage is simply doing what one must do. She would not have thought twice about climbing out that window."

"Did you think twice?" Gavi asked.

"No, and neither did you, Gavriel. All I managed to do was pull the brake. If you hadn't known how to handle the team, we would have perished."

Gavi let go of Millie's hand to pull a branch from the trail. "Perish sounds much more final than merely being killed."

"That's my point," Millie said. "It is final. If God did not have a plan for your life—and for mine as well—He would simply have let us perish."

"We were not the only living souls on that stage," Gavi pointed out. "Perhaps it had nothing to do with me at all. I just don't think I am important enough for Him to notice."

"Gavriel Mikolaus," Millie said, "you are driving me mad. He is the God of the Universe, yet He cares enough to watch over the sparrow. Don't you think it a little insulting to Him to say that you are not important enough to care about? He made you. He cares about each heartbeat and every joy or sorrow in that beating heart."

"My dreams," Gavi blushed, "are impossible."

"Nothing is impossible with God," Millie said firmly. "Have you asked—"

135

# Millie's Great Adventure

"Millie, Millie, Millie!" Fan was running down the path toward them. "A bear et up a pig in Lambertville!"

"The bear did not 'et', it ate," Millie said. "Where did you hear this?"

"Reverend Lord said so. He went baptizing babies there yesterday, and he saw it himself!"

"He saw the bear?"

Fan frowned up at her. "Millie, are you paying attention? He saw what was left of the pig that the bear ate. Lambertville's not too far away. Is that bear coming back here?" There was just one bear in the Kankakee as far as Fan was concerned, a huge black bear with a blaze on his chest. She still woke crying from her dreams about the beast.

"Twenty miles is a long way for a bear," Millie said. "I see no reason why he would come to Keith Hill."

"Other than the smokehouse." Millie frowned at Gavi's remark but she went right on. "It must smell pretty good if you like fish."

"Bears like fish," Fan said, her eyes huge. "Let's go practice with the musket, Millie." The little girl was determined that if the bear ever came to Keith Hill, sister Millie would be ready. She carried the heavy musket for Millie and Ru when they practiced, and counted the holes in the target when they were done. The more holes in the fictitious bear, the safer Fan felt.

"Very well." Millie sighed. She would gladly have avoided the smelly smoke and powder if she could. "But only if Jaz and Annis will give up their walk." To Millie's dismay, it took Fan no time at all to convince the little girls that they would rather feed their baby dolls.

Ru took the musket down from the pegs on the wall while Millie got the powder horn and shot bag out of the cupboard.

136

"How long a shot can you make?" Gavi asked.

"That's what I want to find out," Ru said. "In theory, I should be able to hit the brute from there." He indicated the stump of a tree that had been lost in the storm. "I wouldn't want to be much closer to a bear."

Fan set up the target by the corner of the smokehouse while Ru prepared the musket. When she was behind the firing line again, Ru raised it to his shoulder. The musket roared and blue smoke belched.

"You missed," Fan said.

Ru handed the musket to Millie. "That's the problem with theory. There are always unexpected elements to figure in. You don't know how humiliating it is that you are the better shot, Millie."

Millie wasn't exactly happy about it either. Perhaps Fan was right—it was all in the eyes. Though Millie read a great deal, Ru spent every spare moment poring over books or schematics, his nose inches from the paper. Millie had considered more than once suggesting that he be fitted for spectacles, but she knew there was no money for such things just now. Ru seemed to know his limitations as well as Millie did, and though he made a pretense of practicing, he never took more than one shot before handing over the musket.

Millie measured the powder carefully, using a little more than she normally would. Powder and shot were not inexpensive, but each time Millie tipped the powder horn or reached into the shot bag, there was more than enough. She might have thought the Keiths were experiencing a miracle to rival the widow's oil in the Bible story if she hadn't seen Wallace refilling them when he thought no one was watching. She finished her preparations and raised the musket.

"Pretend he's standing up," Fan said. "Like this!" She raised her arms and snarled to illustrate. It did seem to help Millie's aim to pretend the paper was the blaze on the black bear's chest. She sighted down the barrel and pulled the trigger.

To Fan's dismay, it took her three shots to gauge the powder and distance correctly.

"Good!" she said when Millie hit the target at last. "I knew you could do it, Millie!"

Though the shorter days brought more rest for Stuart and Ru, Marcia and Millie seemed to work twice as hard. They had as much to do each day, and fewer hours of light in which to do it. Millie took on extra chores as well, to allow Adah and Zillah time to work on their gowns for the Winter Social.

Adah was altering one of Millie's old gowns, and Zillah was using a gorgeous blue silk that had been Marcia's. There was very little fabric to waste in either one, so the girls spent hours poring over magazines and discussing sleeves, darts, and hems, and asking their mother's advice before the scissors touched fabric. When the styles had been chosen, they sighed over the lack of new buttons and bows. Marcia dipped into the carefully hoarded money from the sale of Glory and her filly, and sent Millie to the Mercantile to purchase these, as well as thread, as a surprise.

"Ready, Millie?" Cyril asked as she tied on her bonnet. "Mamma said Fan and me could go too, if you allowed it."

"Of course," Millie replied. "I would love the company."

"Hallelujah," Cyril said, "today is the day."

"The day?"

"For the vengeance of the Keiths," Cyril thundered, waving his arms like a tent preacher. "And here she comes now."

Fan tripped into the room. Her hair was neatly braided and her face scrubbed clean. She wore her prettiest bonnet, the one with a bow, and the flowers on her dress brought out the blue in her mischievous eyes. She cradled a baby doll in one arm. If it hadn't been for the sprinkling of freckles on her nose and the bare toes peeking out from under her pantalets, she would have looked a perfect little lady.

"Why, Fan," Millie said, "isn't that Annis's doll?"

Fan nodded. "She said I could play with it. Come on, Millie. We don't want to be late!"

"Late for what?" Millie asked.

"For the marble game," Fan said, as if Millie should have known.

"Fan's fixing to win back Don's Indian marble," Cyril explained, "and teach John some humility to boot."

"I've got Cyril's red agate shooter," Fan said, digging in her apron pocket to prove it.

"What if you lose the marble?"

"I won't lose," Fan said grimly. "I'm a real good aim, and my hands are strong, too. I've been milking Belle two times a day!"

"I see," Millie said. "And you have been practicing playing marbles in the barn?"

Fan nodded.

"All she's gotta do," Cyril said, hitching up his pants, "is trick 'em into letting her play."

Fan and Cyril talked marbles all the way into town, but they pulled Millie to a stop before they reached the Monockers' store. "If they see me, they will figure something is up," Cyril said. "On account of she's got my marble.

I'm going to duck around and go in the back. I'll watch from the window."

Millie couldn't help but feel a little odd as they approached the group of boys squatting in the dust in front of the Mercantile, as if she were part of some sinister plan or a revolutionary plot. She recognized many of the boys from Sunday school, but others she had never seen before — sons of the owners of the boats that plied the river or boarders at Mrs. Prior's hotel. She had a sudden urge to warn them, to shout "put your marbles away!" But before she could open her mouth, Fan, the Vengeance of the Keiths, let go of her hand and tripped over to them.

"Hey," Fan said.

"Hey yerself," a boy in blue suspenders replied.

"Can I play?" Fan asked, pulling the shooter from her pocket. "I've got a marble."

"That's Cyril's shooter," Bill Chetwood said. "Does he know you have it? Don't let her play, Toby."

"I'm sure Cyril knows she has it," Millie said, but no one but Fan noticed the warning. She frowned at Millie over her shoulder, then turned back to the boys.

"You know how to play?" Bill asked. "If you don't knock a marble out, we could win your shooter. We could keep it."

"For good?" Fan said. "But I get to try to shoot first?" Bill scratched his head, unsure of what to do, but Toby wanted the red agate marble Fan held in her hand.

"Let her shoot once," he said. "What could it hurt?"

"I'll be back for you as soon as my shopping is done," Millie said, and she made a hasty retreat to the Mercantile. Inside she found Cyril peering out the window from behind a row of canned goods. "John's not here yet," Cyril said, as he watched Fan set the baby doll against a post and kneel beside the marble ring.

Fan bit her lip and squinted one eye as she put her knuckle to the dirt. The mass of marbles in the center of the ring exploded, one or two rolling out of the larger circle. The boys glanced at one another as Fan picked them up and dropped them in her pocket. Millie couldn't hear their words through the glass, but their expressions said enough.

"Whooo-whoo-eee, she's got 'em now," Cyril crowed.

Millie left him to his spying and gave Mrs. Monocker her order.

Cyril was still pasted to the window when she came back with her purchases neatly wrapped in brown paper. "She's cleaning 'em out, Millie!" he said in awe. "I knew she could, but dawgone, look at her go!"

Millie leaned far enough to look over his shoulder.

Fan was still shooting. Apparently she had not missed yet. Her shooter hit a larger marble, just knocking it out of the ring. Fan picked up both the marbles.

"That was close!" Cyril said. "She's gettin' tired."

"What happens if she doesn't knock it out of the ring?" Millie asked.

"If my shooter stays in the ring, anyone who knocks it out can keep it. Let's go, Millie. I'll go out back and meet you down the street."

"Fan, we must be going now," Millie said as she stepped out the door.

"Awww," Fan said, standing up and dusting off her dress. "I guess I have to go."

"Don't forget your doll," Millie said.

"Hey," Toby said, "you can't leave with our marbles!"

"I won them fair and square," Fan said, hugging the doll. Toby doubled up his fists, but Bill caught him by his suspenders.

"You cain't hit a girl," he said.

"That's right," Fan agreed, putting her nose in the air. "You can't."

"Hey!" Cyril skidded around the corner. "John's comin'. He was just late. Give them back their marbles, Fan. All of them."

"Cyril Keith, what are you doing here?" Bill asked.

"No time for that!" Cyril turned to the boys. "You been letting him win all your marbles for weeks. Now's the time to do something about it. You gotta get him to let Fan play. And nobody lets on." The boys looked at one another.

"Deal," Toby said, spitting at the corner of the porch. "Give me my marbles."

"Now you guys start the game," Cyril said, grabbing Fan's hand. "And give her a couple of marbles back so she can practice."

Cyril dragged Millie and Fan back into the Mercantile and behind a shelf of dry goods. "That's John," Cyril said. "He's comin' down the street with that other feller." Millie started to look but Cyril turned her away. "Pretend you're looking at these cans. Don't even look up. He'll feel it."

The door of the Mercantile opened and closed.

"Did he come inside?" Millie whispered.

"No, it's just some back-east dandy," Cyril said. "Keep looking at the canned peas. Put some marbles down, Fan," Cyril said. "I'll show you one thing you can do different when you knuckle down."

"*Millie Keith?*" The voice sent chills down Millie's spine. She spun around, and blue eyes met her own.

"Char—" Millie took a step backward, and her boot came down on the marbles. She flailed wildly, trying to keep her balance, but the room spun around her. "Leee-eee-eek!" she managed as she went over backwards.

CHAPTER

11

# Heroism and Humility

*Do nothing out of selfish ambition
or vain conceit, but in humility
consider others better
than yourselves.*

PHILIPPIANS 2:3

*G*ive her air!" It was Charles's voice, and Charles's face above her.

"She fainted!" Mrs. Monocker said. "I've got some smelling salts. Here, wave these under her nose."

"I didn't faint, I—"

"Heaven's teapot, what's happening?" Mrs. Prior pushed her way through the gathering crowd.

"Millie took one look at this fellow and fainted dead away!" Mrs. Monocker declared.

"I didn't faint!" Millie insisted, struggling to her feet. "I . . . toppled."

"Toppled, eh?" Mrs. Prior folded her arms and looked Charles up and down. "This must be the infamous *Mr. Landreth!*"

Charles's eyebrows went up. "Indeed," he said, bowing slightly. "My reputation precedes me!"

"So." Cyril stepped forward. "You're the guy who broke my sister's heart."

"My heart isn't broken!"

"It's her head," Fan agreed.

"Sit down, dear," said Mrs. Prior, pulling the lid onto the pickle barrel. Charles lifted Millie onto it; then he turned to her brother.

"You must be Cyril." He extended a hand. Cyril shook it solemnly. "I've heard a lot about you. Now I think we should get Millie home," he said. "She has a nasty bump on the head. Where can I rent a carriage?"

"We'll have to walk," Cyril said, "or borrow Dr. Chetwood's rig."

"Dr. Chetwood is making calls in the next town," Mrs. Prior said. "It's shank's mare or nothing."

"We can't leave yet anyway." Cyril looked at Millie pleadingly. "You're not even bleeding, Millie!"

"I think I will be fine if I just have a moment to sit quietly," Millie said.

Fan was staring up at Charles as if he were a creature from a fairy tale, but Cyril grabbed her arm and pulled her outside.

"Marbles," Millie explained.

"Marbles?" Charles's eyebrows had still not traveled down to their usual position. "Has someone lost theirs?"

"Someone is about to," Millie said. "And more than one person, if Fan has anything to do with it." She hopped down from the pickle barrel, and Charles took her arm to steady her, even though she didn't need it. He tipped his hat to Mrs. Monocker and Mrs. Prior, who were still glaring at him, as they went past.

"Oh, my goodness," Millie said. "That's John?" Fan was nose to nose with a small mountain. He had to bend almost double to face her. He was large in every way possible, bursting-through-his-boots large, popping-out-of-his-overalls large. His hands were the size of coal scuttles. "Cyril," Millie whispered as she reached the edge of the crowd, "that's not a boy."

"He's only thirteen," Cyril said. "Shhh."

John's lip curled in a sneer. "Girls can't play," he said, turning away.

Fan had a death hold on Annis's dolly. Her face was pale. "Yeah?" she said. "That 'cause you're afraid?"

John turned back. "All right, pipsqueak. I'll let you play. But I'm not as stupid as I look. You think I don't know a setup when I see one?" Toby looked at Cyril nervously. "If Cyril Keith's behind it, I know what you want." He pulled out Don's Indian-made marble and set it in the ring, grinding it in to make it harder to move. "Go ahead. Knuckle down."

Fan handed Millie the doll, flexed her fingers, squinted, bit her lip, and shot. There was a crack, and Millie gasped. Fan had shot so hard the agate shooter had shattered when it hit, but the Indian had hardly moved.

"She should get another shot," Charles said. "You pressed that marble in." Everyone could see the hole in the dirt where John had set his marble.

"You got another shooter?" John asked.

Fan looked around. She had given all the shooters back, every one of them. Bill shook his head slightly. No one dared to lend her another. Not with John looking right at them.

"Didn't think so. That Indian-made marble's got juju," John said. "I used juju to win it, and nobody's ever gonna win it from me." He reached for his marble.

"Not so fast." Charles stepped forward. "A *gentleman* always assists a lady in distress." He gave the boys a look, and they shuffled uncomfortably. "Might this suffice?" He pulled something from his pocket and dropped it in Fan's hand.

"Thank you," Fan said, amazing Millie by performing a passable curtsy.

"You keep marbles in your pockets?" Millie asked when he returned to her side.

"Better," he said with a wink. "It's a brass anti-friction bearing. I picked it out of the cinders along the train tracks in Philadelphia. You never know when something of the sort might come in handy."

John started to reach for his marble, to grind it in again.

"No." Bill glanced at Charles and gulped. "Play fair. Even if she is a girl."

"Yeah." One by one the boys moved to stand behind him.

"You're contagious," Millie said with a smile.

"Manners and good sportsmanship tend to be," Charles said, "when there are gentlemen present."

Fan knuckled down and shot. The bearing was a brass blur and then the Indian marble seemed to jump out of the ring. The ball bearing was moving so fast that it, too, spun out of the ring.

Fan walked over and picked them up. "It's been very nice playing with you," she said to John. Suddenly the boys were cheering wildly, slapping Fan's back and shaking Charles's hand.

"Hey," Cyril said, "what about me? It was my plan! I taught her everything she knows!"

"Yeah," Bill said, "but it was his marble that won the Indian. Yours shattered."

"Fan!" Cyril caught up with her at the edge of the boardwalk. "Let me see that shooter. Please!" She held it out to him, and he weighed it in his hand. "You could knock anything out of the ring with this," he said in awe. "You're going to be famous!"

"Do you feel up to walking, Millie?" Charles asked, offering his arm again.

"I do," Millie said. "It's time to go home, Cyril, Fan. Mamma will be waiting." They started up the street, leaving the marble players behind. Millie was glad when they were out of sight of the crowd that had gathered at the Mercantile.

"I have something to tell you," Charles said.

"I have something to tell you as well," Millie replied, trying to sound firm.

"Very well." He stopped and looked into her eyes. "I will go first, but you must promise not to change what you were going to say."

"Agreed," Millie said, and they started walking again.

"Pleasant Plains is somewhat lacking in charm," Charles said as they passed yet another clapboard building.

"That's it?" This time it was Millie who pulled him to a stop. "You have come here to tell me my hometown lacks charm?"

"Of course not." His eyes were laughing. "I came here to tell you that I met a man on a train. His name was Jesus. I was praying and pacing and thinking, and there He was. I have no question anymore that you are right. The whole story you told to Laylie about good guys and bad guys. It's true. And since it's true, I had no choice. I have joined the good guys. Jesus is my King."

Millie felt as if lightning had shot through her, from her head to her toes, melting her feet to the ground. She was sure she couldn't move.

"Well?" Charles said, smiling down at her. "What were you going to say?"

"I have decided . . . to remain a spinster," she said.

"A spinster?"

"The kind of spinster that . . . never marries." Millie gulped, then rushed on. "I am better suited to adventure than housekeeping, I'm sure, and . . ."

"Millie." He caught her hand and Millie winced. His hands were smoother than her own, even though they were strong. *Does he feel the calluses, the roughness? I wish I'd thought to put them in my pockets.*

She was suddenly aware that she was in her calico, the kind of material worn by slaves, or the poorest of the poor in the South. *Surely Charles Landreth has never seen a lady*

# Millie's Great Adventure

*dressed like this. What can he be thinking?* Millie tried to pull her hand away.

"Millie, I . . ."

"Hey!" Cyril was watching them with folded arms. "I'm not sure I approve of this. I'm not sure at all."

"Quite right," Charles said, placing her hand back on his arm. "We should be thinking about getting your sister home."

<hr/>

"You will be staying for dinner, of course?"

"Thank you, Mrs. Keith," Charles said. "I would be delighted."

Marcia must have seen Millie's grimace. The thought of serving Charles Landreth dried fish and greens on top of everything else was more than she could bear. "Would you help me in the kitchen, Millie? And you as well, Don?"

Marcia pulled the tin that held the last bit of money from the sale of the horses from the shelf. "I want you to run to the butcher's," she told Don, "and get me a nice roast. And then stop by the Monockers'. I have carrots and onions, but we will want potatoes. Adah, get the canned peaches we were saving for Christmas. We will splurge on flour and make pie."

"What do you need me to do, Mamma?" Millie asked.

Marcia took her hands. "I want you to go in there and talk with Charles. And don't worry about a thing."

"Thank you, Mamma," Millie said, giving her a kiss.

"I'm very thankful to you for the help you gave Millie in Charleston," Stuart Keith was saying to Charles when she returned. "It's not every southern gentleman who would help two slave children escape."

"There are more than you might suspect, sir," Charles said. "Your own relation, Horace Dinsmore, among them. I could not risk compromising your daughter, but as soon as she was gone, I went to him with the truth. I had offered to pay for the children's freedom when your own letter arrived."

"How is Uncle Horace?" Millie asked.

"Still a good man ruled by a bad wife," Charles said. "When he heard that I would be seeing you, he sent a message." He reached into his breast pocket and pulled out a folded note.

Millie's heart ached at the sight of the familiar handwriting.

*Dear Millie,*

*I hope this letter finds you and your family well. I am grieved by the terms on which we parted, and while Isabel still refuses to allow the children to correspond with you, I wanted you to know that although I cannot approve of your actions, I do admire your courage and conviction. It is my sincere hope that we will be able to meet again, to discuss politics or economics. Until that time I will remain,*

*Your Uncle Horace*

"It's practically as good as forgiveness," Millie said, handing the note to her father.

"As close to forgiveness as Horace can come without offending Isabel," Charles agreed.

"And little Elsie?" Millie asked. "How is she?"

"We became quite good friends," Charles said. "I had to have someone at Roselands to bring flowers to, after all. Enna and Arthur are a trial to her, but her nanny and governess watch over her as if she were a princess. It would do no harm for her father to come home."

"And is there word that he might?" Stuart handed the note back to Millie.

"None." Charles shook his head. "What can he be thinking, leaving his child in Isabel's home?"

They spent the afternoon in conversation of a more pleasant vein, Millie and Charles sharing memories of Roselands and Stuart asking questions of both. They were all laughing by the time dinner was announced.

Charles seemed to fit naturally into the family, as at ease around the Keiths' large table as he ever had been at Isabel's. Everyone but Cyril seemed delighted with his company, particularly when he described Fan's triumph over John. They had heard it from Cyril of course, and from Fan herself, but it was somehow funnier when Charles told it.

"My compliments to the cooks," Charles said at last. "This is an excellent roast." Zillah beamed and Adah blushed. "But I can't help but notice that our heroine has not had a bite."

Fan lifted a fork to her mouth, then let it drop. "I can't," she said.

"It's pretty good," Don coaxed. "Try just one bite."

Fan shook her head.

"Fan," Marcia said. "You must remember your manners. Eat what is put on your plate."

Fan lifted tearful eyes to Charles.

"Why, Fan," he said, "I thought this would be a celebration dinner. You are a marbles champion."

"That doesn't matter," Fan said. "Poor Glory. Poor, poor Glory." She started to cry.

"Excuse us a moment," Stuart said, standing up. "Come with me, Fan. Let's go have a little talk."

Marcia excused herself as well, and they took Fan to the parlor.

"Was Glory her calf?" Charles asked Millie when they were out of earshot.

"Oh, no," Cyril said before she could answer. "Glory was her horse. We've been a little short of cash lately. So . . ." He took a big bite of roast and shrugged as he chewed.

Charles swallowed once, then again. "Excuse me," he said faintly. "I need a bit of fresh air."

"Cyril Keith!" Millie stood up. "How could you?"

Cyril opened his eyes very wide. "I just told the truth!"

Millie found Charles on the back porch.

"Was Glory Fan's horse?"

"Yes," Millie said. "Pleasant Plains may not be picturesque, but we do not eat horses. We sold Glory and Esther weeks ago and used the money to buy dry goods for the winter. Mother used some of the money she'd saved to buy a roast for the meal tonight. You can't believe everything Cyril tells you," she said. "He won't lie, but he is not determined that you understand the truth."

"I see. I must say that eases my mind, even if my stomach is still unsettled. The frontier isn't a bit like I imagined it," he said.

"You prefer the South."

"It doesn't matter which I prefer," he said, looking out into the darkness. "My circumstances have changed. My uncle died, but before he did he made a shambles of his business. You have doubtless heard of the banking troubles in the East? The bank that handled my uncle's funds failed. We lost everything. The house was sold, and the slaves, but there was barely enough to satisfy the creditors. The Landreth fortune is gone. And with our fortune went Isabel Dinsmore's favor. She has revealed my part in Luke and Laylie's escape to one and all. I am banished, I'm afraid. If I return, I face prison or worse."

# CHAPTER

# Battles: Inside and Out

*Who is this King of glory? The LORD strong and mighty, the LORD mighty in battle. Lift up your heads, O you gates; lift them up, you ancient doors, that the King of glory may come in.*

PSALM 24:8–9

h, Charles, what will you do?"

"Many young men in my financial situation live off the benevolence of others until their fortunes turn. Isabel has taken that option away from me. The best families will have nothing to do with me anymore."

"I'm sorry," Millie said. "You've lost everything because of me."

"Not quite everything, and certainly not because of you."

"Not everything?"

"My aunt insisted that I keep the dead relatives." Millie grimaced, thinking of the generations of Landreths that had glowered from the walls of Mrs. Landreth's parlor. "They are hidden like fugitives in a shed in Mrs. Travilla's gardens," Charles said. "Disgraced by their descendant who tarnished the family honor."

"And your aunt?"

"She's gone to live in one of the charity homes that she once funded. It's grim and austere, and suits her disposition perfectly. I'm sure she will be happy there. No flowers or feathers or anything fanciful is allowed. They hold weekly meetings for the women from the street, and if one should be saved, they are ready with scissors at their belts."

"Scissors?"

"Yes. They snip off offending decorations so that ribbons and bows won't keep them from slipping through the pearly gates. I wonder sometimes if my aunt will be happy when she reaches heaven."

"I'm sure she will," Millie said. "Surprised, perhaps, but happy. She does love Jesus after all."

# Millie's Great Adventure

They stood quietly for a moment; then Charles went on. "I have always considered myself a man of the world. But I have found the most surprising thing. Everyone and everything I knew was in the South. When they turned their backs on me, I realized how limited my life had been. The rest of the continent was darkness to me — save one spot of light. I knew someone in Pleasant Plains, Indiana. So I came here."

"I'm sorry for your losses, Charles," Millie said.

"Are you still taking credit for my exile?" Charles laughed. "My life didn't change the day I fell in love with you. It changed the day I decided to help those young slaves escape. The day I chose to act upon what I knew was right. That day, my steps turned toward Jesus."

"How did you come to believe in Him? The last time we talked you accused me of believing fairy tales."

"I was on a train headed north and one step ahead of the law, when I picked up your Bible. I had been reading it, as I wrote, but it still was not real to me. I was reading the Gospel of Matthew when suddenly it came over me that my life had changed when I chose to do right — to be a little like Jesus."

Millie smiled.

"Now, don't misunderstand. I know very well that I was not much like Him, and I am still not, but that one action — helping the children escape — set my whole world against me. It came to me as I was reading, that the whole world was against Jesus as well. They crucified Him. What kind of a fairy tale is that, where the hero is beaten and nailed to a cross?"

"It does have a happy ending," Millie said.

"Thank God for that." Charles shook his head. "I had always thought of Christians as weak people who needed to believe that someone else had paid for their sins. People so afraid of death that they had to believe in heaven. I had somehow missed the Scriptures that say that Christians will be persecuted, treated as Jesus was treated. That they would be killed for telling the world the truth, for doing what was right. When I understood that, I knew it wasn't a fairy tale. I had seen it in my own life, and I had a choice to make. I could either be for Him or against Him. I chose Him as my Lord."

"I was praying for you every day, Charles."

"I thank Him every day for sending you to me."

They stood for a long time in the silence.

"It was so beautiful at Roselands," Millie said. "The whole South, really."

"Yes," Charles said. "If only the dreams of the lords and ladies were true, if only it were not built on human suffering and hopelessness. There will be fire and blood across this land if they do not turn from slavery."

"My Pappa thinks so," Millie said. "And Reverend Lord also. But Charles, if you can wake up—surely, surely they can too."

"We can pray. And in the meantime, one newly exiled Charles Landreth must find a suitable profession."

"Pappa always says that he professes to be a Christian, but he makes his living as a lawyer."

"I like that," Charles said. "Since we are now of a similar profession, that makes us colleagues. However, I still need to find a way to make a living."

"You must find Pleasant Plains poor accommodation after Roselands and the South."

"Do you miss it, Millie?"

"I miss the piano," Millie said with a laugh. "I don't think people who have pianos in their parlors quite appreciate

them enough. To have music at your fingertips, any time of the day or night . . . I think when I get to heaven, the first thing God will say is, 'Would you like to play the piano for Me, Millie?' And I will play for a thousand years."

"You have no piano?"

"There are only two pianos in the whole town," Millie said. "One is in the church and the other in the Granges' parlor."

"I can't imagine you living without music."

"I confess, I sometimes play an imaginary piano." She demonstrated, pressing her fingers into the porch rail as if it had suddenly sprouted ivory keys. She ran her fingers up the invisible scale. "I hear the music, and I believe God does too. He knows what I am playing—and it's just for Him."

"I believe you have a sour note," Charles said, frowning at the wooden rail. "Just here." He leaned over to point at a dent in the rail, the exact size and shape of a hammer's head.

"With this type of piano," Millie explained, "appearances do not affect the tone."

"Mamma's serving dessert," Zillah said from behind them.

Millie realized that she was standing quite close to Charles and stepped away quickly.

"Piano lessons," Charles explained, although Zillah had not asked what they were doing.

"I see," Zillah said, although Millie was quite sure that she did not.

Charles inquired about accommodations in Pleasant Plains over cake and coffee. His means were limited, but he refused Marcia's offer of a room, preferring to take room and board at the Union until he decided what to do next.

Charles Landreth soon became a sensation in Pleasant Plains. Everyone knew of Millie's attachment to him, of course, but that did not stop certain mothers from encouraging their daughters to meet him, just in case. The thought of a match with a rich southern gentleman was too much for them to resist, and although Millie knew he was next to penniless, she kept the knowledge to herself. Charles could have saved the money he spent on board, as the first Sunday he appeared in church he was invited to a different home each night of the week.

The whole town was scandalized, shocked, or simply puzzled when the young man accepted a job at Lightcap's Livery Stable. Rhoda Jane offered a room above the stables and all the food he could eat in exchange for helping with the heavy labor.

"It's something of a relief," Charles said, showing Millie his blisters after his first day of work. "I'm not at all sure I could have kept up with the Pleasant Plains social calendar."

A routine was soon established. After the Keiths finished supper, a knock on the door would announce the arrival of Charles, bundled in a coat against the cold. To everyone's delight he offered to read, and his French was exceptional.

"The last time a young feller came around here every night reading to us, he ended up getting married," Fan pointed out. Millie blushed, remembering Reverend Lord's courtship of Celestia Ann.

"This is a totally different situation," Millie said.

"In what way is it different?" Adah asked.

"Charles is reading in French," Millie said. She wished her face would select one shade of pink. It was distressing to have a complexion that was so . . . changeable.

# Millie's Great Adventure

"You must wonder what the apostle Paul would think of the modern world," Charles said to Millie one Sunday after church. "Trains that rush along at breakneck speeds, steamships that can cross oceans in a matter of days. When you remember all of the time he spent walking . . ."

"I expect he would have marveled at the speed at which we can carry the Gospel from one place to another," Millie said. "To say nothing of printing presses and Bibles with his own letters next to the Holy Books of the Torah."

Reverend Lord's sermon on Paul's missionary journeys had been excellent, and a quiet joy was bubbling up inside Millie as she walked with Charles on one side and Rhoda Jane on the other. Stuart had stayed to discuss the sermon with Reverend Lord, while Marcia, Adah, and Zillah met with the Christmas Social committee, but they would all be coming to Keith Hill for a cold dinner just as soon as the meetings were done. Millie had kissed her mother and assured her that everything would be in place by the time company arrived.

She was almost completely happy walking beside Charles as he carried Annis piggyback. Annis's little legs were too short for the journey home from church. Don, Cyril, and Fan ran ahead, with Ru, Gavi, and Rhoda Jane's sisters bringing up the rear.

Mrs. Lightcap walked ahead of them, resplendent in an outfit from her days as Titania in *A Midsummer Night's Dream*. She had started attending church with Gordon while Millie was away, and the congregation had quickly grown used to her eccentricities. No matter what costume she wore, Mrs. Lightcap always sat very straight and still during the sermon.

When everyone else left, she made her way to the front and had a whispered conversation with God. If anyone came too close during her private talk with the Lord, she would turn to them and say, "Can't you see we are practicing our lines?" Now Rhoda Jane kept a close eye on her mother as she flitted from tree to tree, pretending to be a wood fairy and peeking out at them. This delighted Annis, and she kicked her heels against Charles's side and giggled.

"It's almost unimaginable," Millie said, "that the year is 1837 and we have not reached the ends of the earth with the Good News of Jesus Christ. Fan, ladies do not climb trees in their Sunday clothes." Millie pulled her little sister out of the tree and set her on her feet. "I cannot help but think the apostle Paul would be disappointed."

"Disappointed?"

"Think how many people he reached walking and taking sailing ships. There are countless thousands of Christians in the world today—if each one of us lived as Paul lived . . ."

"Perhaps they are not sent as Paul was." Gavi had quickened her pace. "Do you believe God has a plan for each life?"

"Yes, I do," Millie said. *I plan to be a spinster and an adventuress, don't I?* She tried not to peek at Charles, but somehow she couldn't help it. He was looking at her, too, and she glanced away quickly. "I believe we are all sent to make disciples."

"If we are, then something is seriously wrong," Rhoda Jane said. "We could have changed the whole world by now."

"I think many Christians simply don't stop to ask His plans," Millie admitted. "I don't want to live my life that way. I want to live like my parents and Aunt Wealthy—

awake and alive to the Holy Spirit of God every moment of the day."

"Boys," Millie called as they reached the house, "don't track mud inside. I think we should . . ."

"By the pricking of my thumb, something wicked this way comes!" Mrs. Lightcap posed dramatically on the porch, one thin finger pointing across the yard.

"That's the wrong play, Mamma, that's—" Rhoda Jane's words were swallowed by Fan's scream.

A black lump separated itself from the bushes behind the smokehouse and rose to its hind feet. A bear had found its way to Keith Hill.

"Hey!" Cyril yelled. "Get away from there. That's our fish."

"Cyril, get inside," Millie called. "All of you get inside. Maybe it will go away." The bear started pulling at the door with its claws.

"We can't let it eat the fish, Millie," Don said. "We will starve. And it might eat Belle or Inspiration next."

"I said get away from there!" Cyril took off running toward the bear and Don followed him.

"Get the musket, Millie!" Fan cried.

Millie was already moving toward it, pushing Annis, Mrs. Lightcap, and Fan ahead of her. Rhoda Jane and Gavi followed her in the door. For a moment there was confusion as Millie turned back to reach the musket on its peg over the door. Then Rhoda Jane took the girls by the hand and led them out of the way.

Millie pulled the musket off the wall. She dropped the bag that held the musket balls twice on her way out the door.

"Boys! Stay back," she yelled. Cyril was close now, too close, and he was still yelling.

The bear turned to look for him, turning its huge head from side to side.

"Cyril, get back!" Don yelled, trying to pull Cyril away by his suspenders, but Cyril waved his arms and shouted louder.

Millie's hands were shaking as she measured the powder. She was tamping it down when Cyril's presence finally registered in the bear's small brain. The bear turned toward Cyril and Don. Millie lifted the musket to her shoulder, sighted down the barrel, and waited for her shot. The bear started toward the boys, and the musket roared.

Splinters flew from the shed above the bear's back. *Too far away. I have to be closer to make the shot.* She started loading again, as quickly as she could, but the bear would reach her brothers before she was ready. What Don had understood the whole time seemed to sink into Cyril; they started to back away. *Please, God, don't let the bear charge!*

Clunk! A rock smashed into the smokehouse wall.

"Hey!" Charles Landreth was on the bear's left. Even as Millie looked up, Charles threw another rock. The first had clearly been thrown to get the beast's attention away from the boys. This one smacked into the bear's snout as it turned.

"Hey!" The bear swung its head, looking for the new threat. Cyril and Don were throwing rocks now, too, and the bear did not know which way to turn.

Millie raised the musket again. *Too far. That's why I missed last time.* God had given her time for one more shot, and she dared not waste it. In a split second the bear would decide whom to attack, and someone would die. She tried to take a step forward, but her feet wouldn't move. The memory of the smell of the beast, and the feel of its coarse hair as it brushed past her, washed over her, making her shake so hard she could barely hold up the musket.

*I must get closer. David killed a lion and a bear when he was just a boy, but he could not have done it without God. I can't either. Lord, help me!* Her feet were moving now, and she realized she was praying, her voice growing louder with each step. "The Lord your God is with you, He is mighty to save. He will take great delight in you, He will quiet you with his love, He will rejoice over you with singing."

The bear saw Millie now and seemed to sense that she was the greatest danger. Charles and the boys were pelting the bear with rocks, but its beady eyes were fixed on Millie.

"You are too close," Charles called, an edge of panic in his voice, but Millie didn't answer. She had one chance, one shot, and if she did not kill the bear, then someone — Charles or one of the boys — would die. She kept walking, twenty feet, then fifteen. The bear was ready to attack, she could sense it coming. This was as close as she could get.

"Praise be to the Lord my rock, who trains my hands for war." She lifted the musket to her shoulder. "And my fingers for . . ." — the bear reared, roaring a challenge, and Millie sighted down the barrel at the blaze on its chest — ". . . battle!" Millie squeezed the trigger. The musket slammed into her shoulder, and the bear dropped to all fours and charged right at her. Millie dropped the musket, turned, and ran. She could hear the bear behind her, and then feel it, and she heard the screams of her sisters on the porch and Charles's shout — then it wasn't behind her anymore. Millie didn't know why, and she didn't care either. She kept running until she reached the porch, and Gavi wrapped her arms around her.

"It's dead," Gavi said, turning her around so she could see. "You killed it, Millie."

The black heap in the middle of the yard wasn't moving, but Charles approached it carefully anyway. When he was certain it was dead, he nodded to the girls on the porch. Fan took Millie's hand.

"Come on," she said. When they reached the bear, the little girl looked at it for a long time. "It's the same one," she said at last. "It's the same bear." She kicked the carcass. "That's for Bobforshort," she said.

CHAPTER

13

# Blessings and Blizzards

*Blessed is the man who perseveres*
*under trial, because when he has*
*stood the test, he will receive*
*the crown of life that God*
*has promised to those*
*who love him.*

JAMES 1:12

# Blessings and Blizzards

"What on earth?" Marcia pushed her way through the children who had crowded around the bear. "Stuart! Come quickly!"

"It appears that someone has already done all that was necessary, dear," he said, taking his wife's hand.

"Millie. She shot it straight through the heart," Cyril said. "It charged her anyway, but Millie was faster." Marcia turned away, her hand over her mouth.

"Mamma, you all right?" Annis asked, tugging at her skirt. "Mamma?"

"Yes, dear," Marcia said, pulling her hand from Stuart's, and starting toward the house.

"Mamma," Millie said, walking after her. "*Are* you all right?"

"Oh, Millie!" Marcia turned and hugged her. "Sometimes the frontier is so hard for me."

"What Satan intends for evil, God can use for good," Celestia Ann said cheerfully. "Bears are very good eatin'! I'm going to need a skinning knife and Mr. Roe to help me butcher it. Jedidiah, run and get him, won't you?"

The bear was skinned and dressed, Mr. Roe working so skillfully that nothing was wasted. Celestia Ann set to work bartering bear meat for hams, canned goods, and maple sugar. Mr. Monocker traded two barrels of flour for the hide and sent it to the tanners to be made into a rug.

Millie was sure she would never want to shop at the Mercantile again, with the bear head glaring at her from the wall, but the Keiths' pantry was much better supplied for the winter, if winter ever decided to come.

# Millie's Great Adventure

With Charles doing the heavy work at the stables, Gavi walked up to Keith Hill to visit Millie almost every day, bringing Jaz and Jedidiah with her. Rhoda Jane stayed at the station with her mother, who had not spoken since the incident with the bear.

"I've been thinking," Gavi said one afternoon as they watched the little girls brush Inspiration, "that when Rayme arrives we might buy a piece of land, a place where Jaz and Jed can grow up. I could buy some good stock, and we could raise horses."

"I thought you wanted to travel with me," Millie teased. "We were going off on adventures together."

"My heart seems to have settled here, whether I like it or not," Gavi sighed. "I have fallen in love with a whole town, with Pleasant Plains. Besides, I think, my dear friend, that there is another you would rather adventure with. You may have to give up the idea of spinsterhood, however."

"I have seriously and prayerfully been considering that very thing," Millie said.

"Has he asked you again? Are you engaged?"

"No. It's quite confusing, actually. I'm not sure what we are, but he certainly doesn't seem to be courting me the way he did at Roselands."

"It does seem strange," Gavi said, "that he would ask you three times there, with an insurmountable obstacle between you, and not once here. But who am I to talk? I sometimes think it would be easier if God had not given us hearts at all."

"If we couldn't know sorrow, neither could we know happiness," Millie pointed out.

"I think that would be a good plan, if sorrow and joy were more equally distributed. Some people seem born to one and some to the other."

"The suffering we bring upon ourselves by poor choices is one thing," Millie said, "but I cannot believe that God would make someone only to suffer. Not if they were seeking Him. He has good plans for all His children." Gavi sighed, but Millie went on. "Even Job was blessed by God after his terrible season. I'm sure God has blessings planned for you, and they are just around the corner. Gordon will be back with Rayme before long."

Only he wasn't. October passed, and November arrived with cold wind from the north, but there was no word of Gordon or Rayme. The ladies of Pleasant Plains consoled themselves with the thought that Charles Landreth could dance as they finished making their daughters' gowns and unwrapped packages of dancing slippers, fans, and ribbons. It would be the largest Winter Social ever held in Pleasant Plains, with two sleighs instead of one to carry the young people on their midnight ride. Rhoda Jane sewed bells on the harnesses to be used for the team, while fruitcakes were baked and soaked in rum for the adults and candies concocted for the children.

With dark coming so early each evening, Millie rode more often than she walked, racing Inspiration down roads thick with dry brown leaves and walking her slowly on game trails in the marsh. The threat of the bear was gone, and Millie rode alone again, reveling in the freedom.

One afternoon as Millie rode home, she came upon a wagon struggling up Keith Hill. There was a huge wooden box in the back, and the poor horses pulling it struggled with the grade of the road.

"Hello," she called, as she came abreast of the odd little driver. He pushed his spectacles up on his nose and scowled at her. "Are you taking that to the Keiths?"

"Yes, ma'am," the man said. "Mr. Pinkton has already gone up to tell them about it."

"Tell them about what?"

"The pianer." The man indicated the box behind him with his thumb. "It's for a Miss Millie Keith."

*A piano!* Millie's heart skipped a beat. "Aunt Wealthy Stanhope must have sent it," she said, hardly believing the box could contain something so wonderful.

"Nope," the man said. "This ain't from no Stanhope."

"Then who?"

"I ain't at liberty to say. It's a sur-prise."

*Charles. Charles Landreth, of course. I told him how much I missed the piano.*

"Take it back," Millie said suddenly.

"Now, Miss—"

"I am Miss Keith, and I want you to return this piano to the purchaser. I will not accept it. Turn around now, and you will save yourself half the trip." Millie kicked Inspiration into a trot before she could change her mind. Charles was working himself to death at the Lightcaps'. She simply would not let him spend the money on her. Pianos cost hundreds of dollars! Charles needed the money for himself.

"I'll rub down Inspiration," Ru said when Millie rode up. "Pappa wants to see you inside."

Charles was sitting at the kitchen table in earnest conversation with Marcia.

"It was very kind of you," Millie blurted out to Charles, "but I cannot accept such a gift. Particularly not from a young man I am not even engaged to."

Marcia looked at Charles in surprise. "A gift?"

Charles looked as baffled as Millie's mother did. "Gift?" he repeated.

"The piano," Millie said, taking off one riding glove. "It was a lovely thought, but —"

"Millie, I didn't buy you a piano."

"No?"

"I think I would have remembered a purchase like that. As much as I would like it to, my bankbook just will not stretch."

Millie turned and ran for the door. "Wait!" she yelled, but the driver was too far away and couldn't hear. She picked up her skirts and raced after him. "Wait!" she gasped as she reached the wagon. "I changed my mind. I do want it after all."

When Millie and the wagon arrived in front of the house's porch, they found Stuart and Cyril waiting with a tall, thin man in a suit. He lifted a monocle and examined Millie as if she were a rare bird.

"Mr. Pinkton," Stuart said formally, "may I present my daughter, Millie Keith?"

Mr. Pinkton bowed, and Millie nodded graciously. "May I ask what this is all about?" she asked.

"You'll see." Cyril seemed terribly proud of himself. "Ru's gone after Gavi, and you can't know till she gets here."

The box was carried into the parlor. It chimed promisingly when it was set down. Ru ran for a hatchet and pried the lid off the box. "It is a piano!" Don cried from the chair where he was perched in order to look in the moment the box was opened.

"Of course it is!" Mr. Pinkton polished his monocle. "Of course it is," he repeated, as Gavi, Jed, and Jaz were ushered in. "And this must be Miss Mikolaus! I am Arnold Pinkton, and I represent the Eastern Stage Company.

# Millie's Great Adventure

Some months ago, our company received a most unusual letter, containing . . ." He screwed the monocle into his eye, twisting until it held, then pulled some papers from his pocket. "Containing . . ." he repeated, as he closed the non-monocled eye to examine them, "a most dramatic, though poorly spelled, eyewitness account of a runaway stage, the tragic death of one of our drivers, and a heroic rescue."

"My article!" Jed said. "How did you get that?"

Mr. Pinkton opened his other eye. "You are Cyril Keith? I thought—"

"I'm Jedidiah Mikolaus, and I wrote that account of my sister and Millie saving the stage!"

From the corner of her eye Millie saw Cyril start to ease toward the door, but Stuart's hand shot out and caught him by the collar.

Mr. Pinkton began reading aloud. "Dear Mssrs. of the Eastern Stage Company. My name is Cyril Keith, and I just want you to know that my sister and her friend saved you a lot of money, along with saving some lives. They stopped one of your best coaches from plunging down a cliff.

"I think my sister deserves a reward, and her friend does, too. Now what Millie would want would be a piano, and I'm pretty sure Gavi wants a horse. Enclosed is the first-hand eyewitness account of this daring rescue."

He took out his monocle. "An incredible tale it is, too. I couldn't believe it when I read it. It seemed preposterous."

"It was not!" Jed said. "How do you spell that, anyway?" Everyone laughed.

"Now, now." Mr. Pinkton waved the papers. "The truth is often stranger than fiction. Stories started coming back to us from drivers who had heard of the event. I was dispatched to sort out the facts and authorized to provide ample reward if it were true. We at the Eastern Stage Company believe that good deeds should be rewarded. I am here to present one piano to Miss Keith and one mare to Miss Mikolaus. And," he continued, "to congratulate you both on your courage and bravery. The story has been published in many newspapers."

"My story?" Jed whispered. "My story's been published?"

"If you wrote this, then yes. Would you like to see the mare?" Gavi and the boys followed Mr. Pinkton outside to the barn.

"Can we keep the piano, Mamma?" Annis whispered.

"Of course," Marcia said. "It's a gift from God!" She ran her hands over the mahogany case. "Let's just put it there, Stuart," she said, pointing at the place in the parlor she wanted it to stand. The wagon driver helped him move it, and Millie seated herself and ran her fingers lightly over the keys.

"It's a very sweet-toned instrument," Millie said when Mr. Pinkton returned. "I don't know how to thank you."

"It's the stage company who should be thanking you." He beamed. "I am pleased that you are pleased."

"It's too wonderful, Pappa," Millie said that night after Charles and the Mikolauses had gone home, leading the gray mare.

"I don't expect anything is too wonderful for Jesus," Stuart laughed.

Snow began to fall on the evening of December 5, just as Charles started reading the second volume of *The Swiss*

# Millie's Great Adventure

*Family Robinson*. It soon became a blizzard, hard pellets of ice tapping insistently on the windowpanes. The wind howled around the house like a winter wolf, and for the first time Millie began to believe the old men's warnings.

"You had better stay with us tonight, Mr. Landreth," Marcia said. "I wouldn't want you walking home in this storm."

Charles was hesitant to agree, but Stuart convinced him of the wisdom of staying inside until the storm blew past, and he was given a bed in Ru's room. At dawn the next morning the storm was still raging, piling drifts against the house and barn. The horizon blended with the sky, all the same gray-white color. Cyril and Don sat with their noses to the windows imagining sled races, but Marcia would not let the children outside, for fear they would become confused in the storm and get lost.

Ru and Stuart strung a rope from the house to the barn, just to be safe when they went out to feed the animals. Millie was thankful that Stuart had sold Glory and Esther, as the hay and grain might not have sufficed for them and for Inspiration and Belle.

On the third day the rope was under the snow, and the Keiths' front door was completely blocked. The snow fell for a week, until all the world seemed cast in shades of white and gray. Keith Hill had become an island, although instead of ocean all around, it was winter, fierce and deep. It was the great blizzard of 1837.

"What I'm wondering," Fan said, "is if it will ever stop snowing."

"Of course it will," Marcia said. "But remember, there is a blessing in every situation."

"What's the blessing in this one, Mamma?" Adah asked.

Marcia smiled. "First, we are all safe and warm, and second, the boys have more than enough time to make up the lessons they have missed."

Don and Cyril dragged out their books, and Millie assigned reading and recitation. Charles offered to help them with their mathematics. After lessons they played charades, or listened to Charles or Marcia read, and as the snow kept falling, they said many prayers for the safety of friends in Pleasant Plains.

"I wish pirates would appear at Keith Hill," Don said longingly. "Snow pirates that blow along in sleighs instead of sailing ships. We could build a catapult to launch monstrous snowballs at them."

"No, we wouldn't," Annis said. "Mamma would make them tea and tell them about Jesus."

Charles spent a great deal of time talking with Stuart and Marcia about his Bible study. "I wish I had attended Sunday school more often, or paid attention when I did," he said ruefully. "There is so much to learn, so much to understand. Fan knows more of the Bible than I do! Or at least seems to understand more."

"You have just met Jesus," Marcia said with a smile. "You don't get to know someone all at once. It takes time—like falling in love. Some people fall in love slowly with someone they have known since childhood. Others fall in love with someone new." Millie felt Charles's eyes on her and knew she was blushing. She didn't dare look up from her needlepoint.

"In that case, you must learn all about them," Marcia continued, "how they grew up, what they like to do, what their favorite foods and colors are. The more you know about them, the more you love them. Loving Jesus is exactly like that. The more you know about Him, the better you love Him."

"I cannot imagine loving Jesus more than I do now," Charles said.

Marcia smiled. "It is a little bit like knowing someone great—say, George Washington. You may know everything he ever did and still not know the man. One moment you are introduced, you shake his hand, and you know each other. But if you spend time together, if you listen to what he thinks, and tell him what you think, and share happiness and sorrow, then you become one of his intimate friends." She paused a moment, and then went on. "You have just met Jesus. You believe what you have read about Him. Now you must go about becoming an intimate friend. It's not enough to say, 'Yes, I know Him. I met Him once.' He wants you to spend time with Him—all your time. He wants to be your best friend."

Zillah cried herself to sleep the night before the Winter Social. "I hate snow," she sobbed on Millie's shoulder. "It's nasty and white, and . . ."

"I'm sure we will still have a social," Millie said, stroking her sister's hair, "as soon as we can." Zillah's gown hung neatly in her chiffarobe, her dancing slippers beneath it. Her heart had been set on a dance with Wallace, Millie knew. She tiptoed past her sister's door the next morning. "Let her sleep," she whispered to Adah. "She has had a great disappointment."

Zillah did not appear until after breakfast, her nose and eyes still red. Marcia suggested that they have their own Winter Social, so they spent the day decorating cookies, and Millie popped corn to string for garlands. The house was decked in holiday cheer, but as the afternoon wore on,

Zillah still sighed and gazed longingly out the kitchen window. It was dark, even though the sun was still up, because the snowdrifts had covered the windows on the east side, but Zillah gazed as if she could see past the snow and ice to somewhere far away, somewhere warm, where ladies wore dancing slippers every single day.

"Do you remember what Christmas was like in Lansdale?" Ru asked, and soon the whole family was laughing as they asked, "Do you remember the time . . ."

"Did you hear something?" Stuart asked.

"Halloo in the house!"

"Someone's outside!" Millie ran upstairs, her brothers and sisters behind her. Someone was standing just outside her bedroom window, muffled to the ears.

"Come in," Millie cried, opening her window.

He paused to unstrap his snowshoes, then stepped inside.

"Wallace!" Adah clapped her hands as he started to unwrap. "I wondered who was there." Zillah took his coat, gloves, and scarf.

"Is everyone here well?" he asked, looking around the group of eager faces.

"Yes, we are," Millie said. "But perhaps we could move this meeting to the kitchen?"

Wallace realized he was standing in a young lady's bedroom. "Of course," he said. They followed him down the stairs, and Marcia would not let him say a word until he had a cookie and a steaming cup of chocolate before him. The Keiths gathered around, as eager as castaways for the sound of a new human voice.

"It's the worst storm in a hundred years," he said. "It is a blessing that you prepared for the winter. Those families who planned on buying goods at the Mercantile—well, the river is frozen and no boats are getting through. Pleasant Plains is completely snowed in. I am trying to visit as many as possible, to make sure everyone has food and heat."

"Surely you can't go on tonight," Millie said. "You will have to stay with us."

"Yes," Marcia agreed, "we are having a Winter Social."

"I think it might be wise. That is, if you have room to spare?"

There was a new sparkle in Zillah's eyes as they finished their preparations for the evening. Millie helped her sisters with their gowns and their hair, while Marcia prepared a holiday feast. Ru and Stuart moved the couches and chairs out of the parlor to make a dancing floor.

Millie took her place at the piano, but Marcia sat down beside her. "I will play," she said.

"Would you care to dance?" Charles offered his hand and Millie took it with a smile.

Wallace led Zillah to the floor, while Stuart bowed to Adah.

Millie danced until her feet hurt, showing her sisters new steps she had learned in Charleston. Then she went to the piano, and Marcia and Stuart taught them dances that had been popular when they were courting. It was near midnight when Millie collapsed into her bed.

"Millie?" Zillah was tapping at her door. "May I come in? I'm sure I can't sleep." Millie made room for her sister, and Zillah snuggled under the blankets.

"Don't you think Wallace is a good dancer?" she asked.

"I think he dances very well," Millie assured her.

Zillah sighed happily. "I love the snow," she said.

It was almost a week before Pleasant Plains began to dig out from under the white blanket. People brought out snowshoes, skis, and sleighs, and by Christmas Eve almost everyone was able to make it to church. It was a bittersweet meeting, for they learned that Mrs. Lightcap had walked away on the second day of the storm. Rhoda Jane had tried to find her but failed. Emmaretta and Min sat big-eyed and sad beside their older sister while Reverend Lord prayed.

"Is Mother in heaven with Jesus?" Min asked at last.

"Of course she is," Rhoda Jane said, putting her arm around her sister.

"But how do you know?" Emmaretta asked.

"Didn't you see her rehearsing?" Rhoda Jane asked. "Every single Sunday, Mother and God rehearsed in the front of the church, remember? Now rehearsal is over, and Mother is in heaven."

Rhoda Jane brushed away a tear as the strains of "Silent Night" filled the church. The two little girls huddled against their sister while the congregation sang, and Millie's heart was breaking for them. *Lord*, she prayed, *comfort them. Send Gordon home soon.*

Stuart and Ru had pulled the little girls to the meeting on sleds, and after the caroling and punch, Marcia and Millie bundled them up for the ride home.

As they left the church, Fan gasped, pointing at the sky. Brilliant curtains of purple, red, and green danced above them.

"What is it?" Annis asked.

"The aurora borealis," Millie said in wonder. "It must be. I've read about it, but . . ."

"It's more than that." Rhoda Jane picked up Min and held her toward the sky. "Those are the curtains on heaven's stage, and if they would open up, you could see Mother, Jesus, and all the angels in the greatest play of all time."

Emmaretta gazed openmouthed at the heavenly display. "Did Mother get a happy part?" she asked at last.

"Yes," Rhoda Jane said, "a very, very happy part."

# CHAPTER

**14**

# Promises Broken, Vows Made

*Whatever your lips utter you must be sure to do, because you made your vow freely to the LORD your God with your own mouth.*

DEUTERONOMY 23:23

*M*illie made her way across the yard to the barn, her Bible and prayer journal under her arm. Ru had shoveled the path clear of snow frequently, and now it was piled high on either side. Although it was early February, the snow had not yet shown any sign of loosening its grip on Pleasant Plains. Just after Christmas it had warmed enough one afternoon to begin to melt the snow, but it had frozen hard that night, forming a layer of ice as smooth and sharp as glass on top of the snow. The poor hungry deer left bloody tracks when they came to the edge of the pasture looking for willow bark.

Millie and Zillah had watched from an upper window as a pack of wolves pulled down a thin doe, tearing her to bits in an instant, then fighting over the scraps and pieces. The weaker wolves were left to gulp down mouthfuls of bloody snow to ease their hunger. After that day Ru and the twins took turns sleeping in the barn with Belle, Inspiration, and the few remaining hens. They kept the musket loaded and ready and the barn door tightly shut night and day.

The Keiths felt almost as isolated as the Swiss Family Robinson. If Charles had not examined Wallace's snowshoes and then made himself a pair, they would have been. Every few days Charles came trudging up the hill with an empty backpack on his back. Marcia filled it with butter and soft cheese they made from the milk Belle was still miraculously producing, and dried fish and corncakes, and he would set out again, carrying the food to their neighbors. The stories he brought back broke Millie's heart—families in Pleasant Plains forced to eat their farm animals, even mules and horses, and then the grain the animals would have eaten. With no boats on the frozen river and no wagons coming over the roads, there was nothing left on the shelves of the Monockers' store and no way to resupply. Hunger reached into even the most wealthy homes. Money could not buy what was not available. As it was, the Keiths always had something to share when Charles arrived, exhausted and cold, with his empty knapsack. Millie had seen a pistol in his belt, and she heard him telling Stuart about the wolves that followed like gray shadows as he made his way to the more remote homes. She was proud of him and worried as well, praying for him and for her neighbors even as her hands were busy helping her mother.

Millie pulled the barn door shut behind her and stood a moment as her eyes grew accustomed to the dim light. The air in the barn was warmer than the air outside due to the pile of manure in the corner generating heat, as well as the bodies of Belle and Inspiration. Millie patted their noses on her way to the loft ladder. She settled herself into the hay without disturbing the three hens who shared the loft, and then opened her Bible to Psalm 24.

*The earth is the LORD'S, and everything in it,*
*the world, and all who live in it;*
*for he founded it upon the seas*
*and established it upon the waters.*
*Who may ascend the hill of the LORD?*

*Has it been only weeks since Pappa read that verse to us?* Keith Hill had been the Hill of the Lord. He had been watching over them the whole time—if He had not seen fit to have the Keiths prepare a smokehouse full of fish, and then sent

the bear to meet the rest of their needs, they would have been as hungry as their neighbors.

Millie set the Bible aside and opened her journal. There were so many things she wanted to write here but had to store up in her heart instead. The inkwell in her bedroom kept freezing, and her thoughts were too private to write in the warmth of the parlor or kitchen with her brothers and sisters around her. Here, in the privacy of the hayloft, she could at least read the words and pray aloud.

"When I gave You my heart, I never expected You to take it on such a journey, Lord," she said, paging through her journal. "I feel as curious as Fan. What I'm wondering is . . . what could Charles *possibly* be thinking? He's been here for weeks, and he hasn't spoken to Pappa about my hand in marriage. He seemed on the verge of saying something the first day, as we walked home. Has he changed his mind? Lord, You know that waiting drives me crazy. I don't think I can bear it for one more minute!"

"Your mother said I would find you here."

Millie jumped up at the sound of Charles's voice, spilling her Bible and journal onto the hay and bumping her head on the beam above her.

"Very funny," she said, collecting them again as Charles climbed the rest of the way into the loft.

"Funny?" Charles looked around. "Am I the source of your amusement? I don't mind, if it makes you smile."

"I believe I am the source of God's amusement," Millie said. "You have climbed in on the tail end of a conversation."

"And was the conversation about me?"

"I think you may be coming to know me too well, Mr. Landreth," Millie said. "There are certain things I believe I will keep to myself."

"I see," Charles said, seating himself on the hay. "And this is why you are perched with the chickens in the hayloft?"

"I have developed cabin fever," Millie said. "Even the barn is better than the same four walls all day long, day after day. I wish I could see just one daffodil."

"Not even this winter can last forever," said Charles. "That's what I wanted to talk to you about."

Millie's heart skipped a beat. "Are we to discuss daffodils or the particulars of forever?"

He rubbed his jaw. "Daffodils, I'm afraid."

"What! Charles Landreth, I—"

"Please, just listen. I need to give you back to Jesus, Millie." He wasn't looking at her now, almost as if he couldn't bear it. "When I asked for your heart at Roselands, I was thinking only of myself. Of what would make me happy. I have spent my whole life pursuing my own pleasure. What kind of man would ask a godly woman to follow him, when he had not yet learned to pursue God?"

"I love you, Charles."

"I know. And I love you too. But you are still very young, and I set out to win your heart before I had permission from your Heavenly Father or your earthly father."

"Did Pappa say you could not seek my hand in marriage?"

"I haven't asked him," Charles said. "But I know Stuart would approve of what I am saying right now. You have just turned seventeen, Millie Keith. I can't ask you to wait for me. I don't know how long it will be—it could be years. I am releasing you from any commitment I asked your heart to make. And asking your forgiveness for trying to win your affections before I was ready to be the kind of husband God wants you to have." He stood up.

"Charles?" Millie called after him, and he turned. "Have your feelings toward me changed?"

"Yes," Charles said simply. "In this way: I love you better than I did before. I love you enough to want God's best for you, Millie, as you wanted God's best for me. It's cold here. Perhaps you should come inside?"

"No," Millie said, "I want to be alone for a while."

He turned and went down the ladder. Across the yard, the ropes of Millie's old swing hung from the branches of the tree, even though the swing was buried in the snow. *It will be all right with Charles Landreth. It is all right. He belongs to Jesus forever.* The sob exploded from her even though she tried to hold it back. She pulled her kerchief out and pressed it to her face to soak up the tears before they froze on her cheeks. She was still sobbing into the cotton square when her mother came to the barn and found her.

"Millie," Marcia said, pulling her up onto her lap just like a child. "Charles has explained that he must be going as soon as the river is navigable. Your father and I are so proud of him. He is thinking about you, you know."

"I know, Mamma," Millie said. "I am proud of him, too. But I don't know how long . . . Mamma, I'm just not good at waiting. It could be years and years."

Marcia put her arms around her. "God doesn't want you to wait, Millie, mine. He wants you to live."

"But my heart is breaking."

"I know. You cry. Just go ahead and cry. But remember, dearest—Jesus is the Lord, even of broken hearts."

Millie cried on her mother's shoulder until every tear seemed to have been squeezed from her. "Are my eyes all puffy?" she asked at last.

"Yes," Marcia said. "And red, as well. But we may be able to do something about that. Wait here." She returned in a few moments with a handful of snow wrapped in her own clean kerchief. Millie pressed the cold compress to her eyes; then she opened it and used the water melted from her hands to splash her cheeks.

"How do I look?" she asked at last.

"The nose is still a little red," Marcia said, wiping Millie's face with the corner of her apron. "But cold air has been known to cause that. Shall we go in?" They climbed down and walked arm in arm to the house.

Charles had already gone. When he returned in three days, Millie was relieved to find herself calm and composed, even as he announced his decision at the supper table.

"Where will you go?" Stuart asked.

"Chicago keeps coming to mind during my prayer times," Charles said. "And it seems as good a destination as any."

"I remember Chicago," Fan said. "There were flowers and books."

"From Dr. Percival Fox!" Don said.

"He was in love with Aunt Wealthy," Zillah explained, and giggled.

"He was not," Don said, as if defending the man's honor. "He gave us coonskin caps! Say, if you're going to Chicago, you could take him a bear claw necklace."

"Tell him Millie shot the bear," Cyril said. "He'll like that."

"You might ask him if he is allergic to bears before you present it," Stuart added. Millie couldn't help but smile, remembering the round little man who had shared a packet

boat journey with the Keiths. The Percival Fox they had known suffered terribly, both from allergies and severe bouts of pomposity and self-importance. *Has he changed since he gave his life to Jesus?*

"I will carry the necklace and inquire after his health before I present it," Charles assured them.

In early March, a warm west wind swept over Pleasant Plains. The spring melt began and the ice on the river began to groan and pop. The first boats up the river were met by hungry townfolk eager for canned goods, flour, and salted meat. The shelves of the store were stocked once more, and people stopped by to look at the piles of canned goods and barrels of flour, cornmeal, and beans, as if simply knowing they could buy or barter for them made them rich.

On the last day of the month, the Keiths said good-bye to Charles Landreth. Visitors to Pleasant Plains no longer had to take rowboats out to the larger boats in the river, as they had five years before when the Keiths arrived. Now there were docks and a new pier where the river had been dredged.

Charles shook Stuart's hand, and then walked down the pier with Millie, to speak with her alone.

"How do they say good-bye on the frontier?" he asked.

"Keep your powder dry," Fan called after them. "That's what the mountain men say."

Charles shook his head. "That child's hearing is far too sharp." Millie was sure from the way that Adah and Zillah were looking intently at the boat that they, too, were straining to hear every word. "But she may be right," Charles said, taking Millie's hand and bowing to kiss it. "Keep your powder dry, Millie Keith. And may God watch over you."

"And you, Charles. Will you write?"

"No," Charles said. "I'm afraid I would be like a drowning man, grasping at straws. I would hold on to you and wait for your letters, when I should be holding on to God and reading His words." They walked back, and Charles shook Stuart's hand again before he boarded.

They watched until the plank was raised and the boat untied. Charles waved as it started to move, and Millie waved back, then turned away. *Just live. That means putting one foot in front of the other. But how is that possible, when the whole world is swimming in tears and I can't even see the path?*

Stuart took one of Millie's hands, and Marcia the other, as they walked back through Pleasant Plains to the house on Keith Hill.

Millie spent more time than ever before at the Lightcaps'. The sense of loss and of waiting that filled her own life echoed in each heart at the stage station. There had been no word for Gavi from Gordon or Rayme, and Mrs. Lightcap's body had never been found. Wallace believed she had wandered onto the ice of the river and been carried south during the spring breakup.

On May 3, the first stage to fight its way through the snow and mud rolled into Pleasant Plains. The driver carried a letter from Gordon saying he had found Rayme and they were on their way.

"It's dated December 5, the day the storm started," Millie said, after reading Gordon's terse words. "I wonder where they have been, and what they have been up to?"

"And when they will get here," Jedidiah said. "You'd have thought they would have made it by now!"

# *Promises Broken, Vows Made*

It was a month before they had answers to any of their questions. Millie, Rhoda Jane, and Gavriel were on the station porch when Gordon Lightcap stepped off the stage.

"Gordy!" Rhoda Jane was off the porch in an instant. Gordon gathered her in his arms and swung her around, but Millie's eyes were on the young man who followed Gordon out of the coach. His curly black hair was almost long enough to hide his gold earring as he glanced around. His two waistcoats, one of blue and one of yellow, were fashionably cut, his fawn pantaloons and Hessian boots spotless. There was something catlike, almost dangerous, in the way he moved. Millie had seen that style of clothing, that manner before—when she had traveled down the Mississippi on the riverboats. She had never entered the gambling parlors on the upper decks, but she had often seen young men much like this walking the deck.

"Is he a pirate?" Jaz asked, peeking around Millie's skirts.

"That's Rayme," Gavi whispered. "Rayme Romanik."

"Gavriel?" He strode toward them. "Gavriel! Is it you?" He looked her up and down, and Gavi flushed. "Why, you have grown into a beauty!"

"I thought I was a beauty when last we met," Gavi said.

"You were a child."

"I was old enough to marry you, according to our laws."

"This is the new world, Gavi." Rayme smiled and a gold tooth flashed. "With new laws. I knew it even then, even when Grandfather forced me to . . ." He didn't finish the sentence, but turned to Millie. "And who is this charming young woman?"

"Rayme Romanik, I would like to present Miss Millie Keith, a good friend of mine."

195

"Gavriel's friends should be mine as well." Rayme reached for Millie's hand, but she stepped back.

"I . . . I need to care for the horses," Gavi began.

"I'm home," Gordon said, untangling himself from his sisters. "I will take care of them."

"Where are we staying?" Rayme asked, as the driver deposited a bag at his feet.

"We?" Gavi flushed again.

"Of course we, darling. You are my wife."

"Almost your wife."

Rayme caught her hand. "You are an old-fashioned girl, aren't you? Nothing stands between us but a bit of bread that we have not exchanged." He kissed her hand, lingering just longer than Millie thought appropriate. "Everything else is settled. If I had known how beautiful you were, I would have come sooner."

"Rayme." Gavi took her hand back. "It's been so long . . . I need some time to think about this."

"Just like a woman," Rayme said, winking at Millie. "Wants me to woo her and win her, even though we are as good as wed! So, where will I be staying?"

"Let me show you to your room." Rhoda Jane held the door open for him. Millie could tell by the ice in her voice that Rayme had been weighed and found wanting.

Rayme must have sensed it as well, as he raised one eyebrow. "Must I carry my own bag?"

"Not at all." The ice grew thicker as Rhoda Jane picked up the bag. Rayme only laughed. Millie noticed for the first time that his left arm was stiff.

"A card accident," he explained when he noticed her look. "We were snowed in at a little town in Illinois with a man with a passion for poker. It seemed I had the wrong cards, and he had a knife."

"Millie!" Gavi grabbed her arm after Rayme followed Rhoda Jane up the stairs. "You have got to stay here with me. At least for a few nights. My head is spinning!"

"I have a better idea," Millie said. "You will stay with me. Gordon is back now, after all. Gavi, you have no parents to advise you, but I am sure Mamma and Pappa would be only too happy to stand in their place."

It took Gavi less than an hour to decide that staying at the Keiths' was the best plan of action, although Rayme disagreed. "We have only three days, darlin'," he said. "I've been away from the tables longer than I can afford, now that I have a wife and two children to keep."

"All the more reason Gavi should stay with me," Millie said. "It will give her time to say good-bye."

Marcia embraced Gavi when the two girls arrived at Keith Hill and Millie explained the sudden visit.

"Of course you can stay," Marcia said. "As long as you like. I would like to meet this young man myself."

She and Stuart both had their first opportunity that night, as Rayme came calling. He was obviously intelligent and well-traveled. He had an easy laugh and a warm sense of humor. "That wicked old man," he said when he heard that Grandfather Romanik had tried to make Gavi keep house for him. "If I had known that, Gavriel . . . I'm glad you had the sense to run. He didn't take anything from you, did he?"

"If you mean the betrothal necklace, he did not," Gavi said. "I have kept it safe."

"Good girl." Rayme clapped once. "I always knew you had guts and brains as well!" Conversation turned to plans for the future, and Rayme revealed that he was willing to settle down as soon as he made enough at cards. "I do believe in God," he said, when Stuart questioned him. "But I can't say I've read His book. I've never had anyone to read to me, or to teach me for that matter. Now I do." The smile he gave Gavi was warm.

"I don't like him," Adah said, as she helped Millie with the dishes.

"I think he's almost as handsome as Wallace," Zillah sighed. "And he did come here looking for Gavi."

"Gordon dragged him here," Adah said. "He says that he was stabbed with a knife, but I think Gordon had to twist his arm to get him on the stagecoach. And I'm not impressed that he believes in God, either. Satan believes in God, and at least he knows the Bible!"

"Girls!" Millie said sternly. "Rayme is a guest in our home, and I am sure Jesus would want us to show him Christian charity."

"Perhaps he just needs a good example set," Zillah said.

"Perhaps." Millie wiped the suds from her hands, but in her heart she agreed with Adah. She had not seen one thing about Rayme Romanik that she liked.

***

"Is there anything about gambling in the Bible, Millie?" Gavriel lay across Millie's bed, her hands over her eyes.

"No specific verse forbids it, but . . ."

"What am I going to do?" Gavi didn't wait for her to finish. "I want to obey God. And the Bible does say to honor your mother and father. They arranged this marriage for me. I have a responsibility to them . . . and to my people."

"God would not expect you to obey your parents if they told you to do something that was clearly not His will."

"Perhaps God wants to use me to change Rayme. He can't even read the Bible, Millie."

"Do you love him?" Millie asked, sitting down beside her.

"How can I know? I have only just met him again, and . . . he is very different from the Rayme I dreamed of. But Rebekah in the Bible didn't know Isaac when she went to be his wife, did she? That was an arranged marriage, and it was God's plan."

The night before Gavi was to leave with Rayme, he stayed late talking to Stuart and Marcia. "I'll be back with a wagon at dawn," he said. "We will want to catch the early stage." There was an uncomfortable silence in the parlor after he had gone.

"If I were your daughter," Gavi said at last, "would you allow me to marry Rayme?"

"Even if you were our daughter," Stuart said gently, "we could not choose your way for you. We could only give you godly advice. You are a grown woman, and the choice must be your own."

Gavi nodded slowly. "For years I have depended on the fact that my parents chose Rayme for me. I thought it would be simple, but it's not."

"It is not simple," Marcia said. "But you can depend on God to guide you and help you. Through His Word, through advice from us, through the workings of your own heart."

"May I ask your opinion of Rayme then?"

"I believe Rayme has the potential to be a good man," Stuart said carefully. He laid his hand on Marcia's. "God's command is for a husband to love his wife, as Christ loved the church, and lay down his life for her. I would not advise my daughter to marry any man who did not show that kind of love."

"God's command to a wife," Marcia said, smiling up at Stuart, "is that she honor her husband. I would want my daughter to ask herself this: is this a man I will be proud to stand beside? Is this a man that I respect and esteem?"

Gavi turned to Millie, and Millie blushed. "I don't know as much about this as Mamma and Pappa, of course," she said. "I only know that I would look for the same thing in a husband as I look for in my friends. I would want him to be of good character."

"And how do you determine their character," Gavi asked, "if you haven't much time?"

"By what they love," Marcia said. "You can tell what someone has inside by finding out what they love best."

In Millie's room, Gavi sat at the desk with her Bible open before her. "Will you sit up with me and pray tonight?" she asked.

"Of course," Millie said, curling up in the other chair with her own Bible on her lap. Gavi bowed her head, and Millie could see tears shining on her cheeks as she prayed.

Millie opened her Bible and it happened to fall open to the Song of Songs. "Let him kiss me with the kisses of his mouth—for your love is more delightful than wine. Pleasing is the fragrance of your perfumes; your name is like perfume poured out . . ." *Surely this was not the song of a girl who had to rescue her young man, or one who had to teach him how to follow God! Heavenly Father, Millie prayed, let Gavi find a love like this! Let her have the Song of Songs. Direct her footsteps and let her find Your best for her life. You have promised to give wisdom to any who ask. Lord, give her wisdom now. Show her that You do have*

_good plans for her life. . . ._   Millie prayed, read her Bible, and
prayed again as the hours dragged by.

"Millie, wake up." Gavi was shaking her shoulder.

"Huh?" Millie realized with horror that she had been
asleep, face down on her Bible. This was exactly how the
disciples must have felt when Jesus woke them from their
sleep in the Garden of Gethsemane. There was no more
time to pray, no time to talk. "Gavi, I'm so sorry—"

"Don't be," Gavi said. Her face was calm. Millie looked
at the bag already packed on the bed.

"Are you sure, Gavi?"

Gavi just smiled. "We let you sleep through breakfast,"
she said. "Everyone is waiting for us downstairs."

"Let me take that for you," Rayme said, as Gavriel came
down with her bag.

Gordon Lightcap had driven the wagon from the station.
He stood waiting by the door, while the Keiths all gathered
around Gavi, Jaz, and Jed.

Gavi looked around at them all. "I just need to take out
one thing first," she said. She reached in her bag and pulled
something out. Gold flashed as she shook the coins. Then
she tossed the necklace on the table.

"What are you doing?" Rayme asked. "Gavriel? What
are you doing?"

"A lifetime is a long time, Rayme Romanik," she said. "I
want to know what is in your heart. You may have me or
the gold. But not both."

Rayme shook his head. "This is madness. We can have
both. And the gold is mine. It comes from my family!"

"Right at this instant, it is mine," Gavi said. "And it
remains mine until our ceremony is complete. I choose to
give it to the Keiths."

"It's a fortune," he said, looking at the coins. He shook his head once, then picked up the necklace.

The color drained from Gavi's face. "You will release me from my vows."

"You are released," he said, and went out the door.

Everyone stood in stunned silence for a moment, then Ru stepped over to Gordon. "I'll drive the wagon to the station," he said, and slapped Gordon's shoulder as he went out the door.

"Right," Gordon said. "Right." He cleared his throat. "Miss Mikolaus, I want you to know that I am a man who keeps his promises. I promised that I would find your husband."

"You found him, Gordon," Gavi whispered, "but he didn't want me."

"Yes, he does," Gordon said. "You were looking to the wrong man, that's all. Rayme Romanik is a fool, and no kind of husband for you." Everyone in the room seemed to freeze, Marcia with her hand to her heart, Zillah starting to rise from her chair. "I'm . . . I'm convinced that I am the man for you, and I'm asking you to let me convince you of it."

Cyril's mouth was hanging open. Don smacked the back of Cyril's head, and his mouth closed with an audible pop.

"Do you mean you want to come calling on my sister?" Jed folded his arms.

"That's just what I mean," Gordon said, flushing.

"What do you think, Mr. Keith?" Gavi asked.

Stuart rubbed his chin. "Well," he said, "a proper courtship can take some time. I assume you will be moving back to Keith Hill for the duration?"

"Gavi," Gordon said, "if you don't give me an answer I'm gonna fall over."

"Yes," Gavi said simply. "The answer is yes."

"Well," Marcia said. "I think I need some help cleaning up the breakfast things. Girls? Shall we?"

Stuart ushered the boys out the opposite door, leaving the young couple alone.

The kitchen was buzzing with whispers and giggles as Zillah peeked through the door to the parlor. "But doesn't she love Rayme, Mamma?"

"I think our Gavi's heart has been turned toward another for quite some time," Marcia smiled.

"Do you mean Gordon?" Adah asked. "Then why didn't she answer him right away? Why didn't she just say that she would marry him?"

"It won't do him any harm to court, nor her to be courted," Marcia said with a smile. "Come away from the door, Zillah. Ladies do not eavesdrop."

Gavriel became Mrs. Gordon Lightcap in July of the next year. The wedding was held at Keith Hill, in Ru's rose garden. Princess Jasmine was the flower girl, scattering petals before the bride, while Gordon looked pale and serious in a suit borrowed from Wallace.

Just as Gordon kissed his bride, a huge yellow-and-black swallowtail butterfly floated into the garden, glided past the bride and groom, then followed the summer breeze over the treetops.

"A butterfly at a wedding is good luck," Mrs. Roe said, dabbing a tear. "Don't you think?"

But Rhoda Jane was staring after it. "A butterfly at Gordon's wedding . . . Isn't that what Mother said? A yellow butterfly!"

# Millie's Great Adventure

"Perhaps Jesus told her about it during one of their talks," Millie said with a smile. Her own heart was full of happiness for her friends, but still there was a tiny ache, and she had not heard from Charles Landreth since he left. He had been as good as his word, but that did not keep Millie from praying for him each and every night.

In the fall of that year a letter came for Millie, not from Charles but from Wealthy Stanhope. Millie read her aunt's words, and then read them again prayerfully, standing in the graveyard over the stone where she had buried her will.

"It is a good thing the world was frozen that winter, Lord," Millie said, "or I would have dug up this rock and flung it in the river. I want You to know something, Lord. I choose You. I choose You even if I never see Charles again."

She looked at the letter. Something about it whispered of faraway places and sent tiny shivers down her back. *Here there be monsters.* But here also was adventure and the chance to do what Millie was more and more convinced she was created for—to tell the lost and dying about Jesus. Finally she took the letter from Aunt Wealthy to her parents.

"I know you said you would never let me leave home again, Pappa," Millie said, "but this is different. Aunt Wealthy needs my help. May I read it to you?"

Stuart nodded.

*My dearest Millie,*

*I have a wonderful opportunity to spread God's love in the French Quarter of New Orleans. There are many free blacks there as well as mulatto girls. You know the only kind of life*

*that is available to them—society will not allow them to
marry, and they must support themselves in some manner.
The poor things end up being mistresses at best. A dear friend
of mine has opened an underground school where they will
learn of Jesus, and learn various trades as well. There is an
immediate opening for a piano teacher. If you would prayerfully consider—*

"No." Marcia stood up. "One year was enough, Millie. I
couldn't bear to have you leave again."

"Dear." Stuart took his wife in his arms. "Perhaps Millie
is called to missionary work, like your Aunt Wealthy.
Wealthy would never have been happy staying in one
place."

"I know I'm called, Mamma," Millie said. "God is calling
me to New Orleans to work with Aunt Wealthy. Didn't you
tell me to put one foot in front of another? To live for
Jesus? Jesus' heart is breaking for those girls. My heart is
breaking for them, too."

# EPILOGUE

# *Epilogue*

*Y*ou've been practicing," Millie said with a smile.

Joy Everlasting Lord looked up at her with big blue eyes and nodded solemnly. "Yeth, Mith Keith," the little girl lisped. She had her first loose tooth and simply could not keep her tongue from wiggling it, even long enough to speak.

"Play it again, dear." Millie stepped to the window and looked out across the green lawn to the meadow. When she had returned to Pleasant Plains from New Orleans, she had insisted on earning her own way in the world. Claudina and Lu and Helen had married and were busy with their own homes and families, and Marcia had all the help she needed. Even if Millie had been run out of the South once again, she was determined to send the money she earned to certain individuals who would know how to spend it for the Lord. Little Joy had been the first student to enroll for the piano classes Millie now offered. Pleasant Plains had grown wider, taller, and altogether more substantial, with two-story brick buildings and tree-lined lanes. There were more than enough music students for three teachers, but the Lords' daughter was her favorite of all.

It was so simple, so peaceful here after the tensions in New Orleans. Millie frowned. A horse raced across the meadow, a bareback rider leaning low over its mane. Even if the breakneck speed had not, the wild black curls gave away the rider's identity.

"Jaz ith in twouble again," Joy said solemnly. The horse reached the pasture gate, and Millie caught her breath. The mare cleared the gate as if flying were as natural as running when the ten-year-old was on its back. Jaz glanced over her shoulder as they flashed past the window, and Millie was sure Joy was right. Jasmine Mikolaus was in trouble once again.

"Perhaps she has just come to see Annis," Millie said hopefully. "Play that last scale for me again." Joy had not finished the scale when Jasmine Mikolaus burst into the room, her face rosy with excitement.

"Millie!" she gasped. "Hide me!"

"Hide you?"

"He's right behind me," the girl wailed. "He said he was here for Millie Keith, and he talked like the man who came from New Orleans with the warrant for your arrest that time. I . . . I tried to stop him, Millie. I flung a rock at him."

"And he chased you?"

Jaz nodded, her eyes huge and frightened.

"He's coming here for you, Millie."

Millie felt her temper rising. Stuart and Wallace had taken care of the warrant. They had been assured that the case would not be pressed if neither Millie nor Aunt Wealthy returned to the South. What kind of man frightened young girls? What kind indeed! Footsteps thudded on the porch.

"You gotta run, Millie," Jaz pleaded. "They'll drag you back and hang you for sure this time!"

"We'll see about that!" Millie snatched up the first thing that came to hand, her purple parasol, just as a rap sounded on the door.

"Stay behind me, girls." She walked to the door and jerked it open. The man on the porch had just put his hand to his brow, where his hat was pulled down low. Millie placed the silver tip of her parasol directly on the third button of his vest.

# Epilogue

"Stop right there, sir," she said. "I would not have opened the door if I had not decided to see what kind of man chases small girls — and to show you exactly what I think of this behavior." She gave a sharp push with the parasol, and he stepped backwards, tripping over the welcome mat and tumbling down the steps. Millie was just pushing the door shut when she caught sight of his face. She pulled it wide open again.

"Charles!"

Charles Landreth stood up, brushing dust from his once impeccable jacket.

"Dr. Charles Landreth," he bowed. "At your service, and exceedingly glad you were wielding your umbrella rather than a musket." Millie started down the steps, but Charles waved her back. "I'll come up there, if you don't mind."

"Of course," Millie said. "Come in." Then remembering the little girls hiding behind her, she called, "It's all right. Charles Landreth is an old friend of mine. My students," Millie explained, "Joy Lord and Jaz Mikolaus."

"I believe I have met both of them before," Charles said, taking off his hat to reveal a nasty bruise on his forehead. "Though they may not remember me. Joy was just a baby."

"A baby!" Jaz said. "She's already six years old!"

"It has been a very long time." Charles's eyes went to Millie. "I heard that one of the Keith girls was married, and I thought perhaps . . ."

"Zillah married Wallace last spring," Millie said. "You have become a doctor?"

"You can blame it on Percival Fox," Charles said. "I did attempt to deliver the bear claw. He was, as you suspected, allergic, but he sent it to someone who would appreciate it and invited me to spend the night. He was fascinated by my tales of the Keiths on the wild frontier. I in turn was fascinated by his medical practice the next day. I followed him through the tenement houses, helping the sick and giving comfort to the dying. For a man with allergies, he does amazing work for the Lord. He invited me to stay the week. I ended up staying five years and becoming a doctor myself."

Millie started to laugh, and soon found she was laughing so hard she had to sit down on the chair Charles pulled up for her.

"Dr. Percival Fox was the very first person I led to the Lord," she explained, "although it happened in a roundabout way. It may even have been more Aunt Wealthy's doing than mine, but still . . ."

"Still, God has an amazing sense of humor," Charles said, "which brings me to the reason for my visit. I have been praying for a wife, and . . . your name keeps coming up. I can't pretend that I have traveled here for any other reason."

Millie wiped the tears of laughter from her eyes.

"Perhaps I shouldn't have sprung it on you so soon," Charles said, and after a long moment he asked, "Could you tell me what you are thinking?"

"Of daffodils," Millie said happily.

"Daffodils?"

"Have you ever noticed?" She took his hand. "They are the very first flowers to greet the spring."

# Will Millie marry Charles at last?
# What exciting changes will the future bring?

*Find out in:*

# MILLIE'S RELUCTANT SACRIFICE

Book Seven
of the
*A Life of Faith:
Millie Keith* Series

*Available at your local bookstore*

**\* Now Available as a Dramatized Audiobook!**

# Do you want to live a life of faith?
## Are you interested in having a stronger devotional life?
### *Millie's Daily Diary* can help you!

## MILLIE'S DAILY DIARY
### A Personal Journal for Girls

### SPIRITUAL VITAL SIGNS

When it comes to the human body, vital signs (like your pulse and blood pressure) measure your physical health. Likewise, when it comes to your spiritual health, there are vital signs that measure the state of your spiritual life. Are you walking in faith, hope and love? Are you spending time with God? Are you feeling resentment or hardness of heart toward anyone? Is the fruit of the Spirit growing in you? This is the place to record the results of your regular, spiritual checkups.

Full of beautiful color photos of Millie, this journal has the unique feature of tabbed sections so that entries can be made in different categories — daily reflections, prayers, answers to prayer, favorite Scriptures, goals & dreams, and more.

*Available at your local bookstore*

# Collect our other
# *A Life of Faith* Products!

# Collect all of our Violet products!

## A Life of Faith: Violet Travilla Series

# — ABOUT THE AUTHOR —

*M*artha Finley was born on April 26, 1828, in Chillicothe, Ohio. Her mother died when Martha was quite young, and Dr. James Finley, her father, soon remarried. Martha's stepmother, Mary Finley, was a kind and caring woman who always nurtured Martha's desire to learn and supported her ambition to become a writer.

Dr. Finley was a physician and a devout Christian gentleman. He moved his family to South Bend, Indiana, in the mid-1830s in hopes of a brighter future for his family on the expanding western frontier. Growing up on the frontier as one of eight brothers and sisters surely provided the setting and likely many of the characters for Miss Finley's *Mildred Keith* novels. Considered by many to be partly autobiographical, the books present a fascinating and devoted Christian heroine in the fictional character known as Millie Keith. One can only speculate exactly how much of Martha may have been Millie and vice versa. But regardless, these books nicely complement Miss Finley's bestselling *Elsie Dinsmore* series, which was launched in 1868 and sold millions of copies. The stories of Millie Keith, Elsie's second cousin, were released eight years after the *Elsie* books as a follow-up to that series.

Martha Finley never married and never had children of her own, but she was a remarkable woman who lived a quiet life of creativity and Christian charity. She died at age 81, having written many novels, stories, and books for children and adults. Her life on earth ended in 1909, but her legacy lives on in the wonderful stories of Millie and Elsie.

# Check out our web site at www.alifeoffaith.com!